TWISTED TALES FROM A MURDEROUS MIND

To Alix,

a delightful new friend!

with much appreciation,

Linda Ungar

By Linda Ungar

TABLE OF CONTENTS

HER LAST WILL

"I can't believe that I have you two together again." Amelia, withered and pale, smiled as she settled back on to her pillows. Amelia, now confined to bed, was a victim of time. Time the master thief – silent, never seen. Only when it passes is it apparent what has been lost. "Your being here brings back so many memories. Do you remember how it was when we were all girls? Poor Daddy, what a bother we were in those days, always running to him with our troubles, and he left alone when Mommy died after catching your chicken pox. Of course you girls were too young to remember."

"But you always remind us, don't you Amelia?" sniffed Rose. Her resolve to remain calm, shattered. Amelia continued as if nothing had been said. "Why I don't know how that man put up with all that squabbling going on! Mommy swore you two fought in the womb. She'd say it was the only explanation for all the turmoil she felt inside. Charlotte, you really were wicked hiding that doll Rose got for Christmas when you were six...on the day she got it, too!" Amelia's eyes narrowed as she twisted her head to smile at Charlotte.

"You still remember that? Hmm...I don't know how long it's been since I've given that incident a thought. You certainly have an amazing memory Amelia."

"It's part of my life and I'm not about to relinquish a moment of it, unless I absolutely have to. Though it looks to me as if I don't have much longer. Knowing that makes my memories even more precious."

"Oh hush now!" Rose said anxiously, and went about adjusting Amelia's blanket and pillows, as if that could put everything into its proper order.

"I don't like to hear you talk like that either," agreed Charlotte. "You just have to be patient, you'll begin to feel stronger before too long. I know it's hard waiting for what you want. You never did learn to have any patience, did you?" She turned her head quickly away from Amelia's fixed gaze, blinking back the tears, her eyes searched the room intently.

"Well, I see you haven't changed anything in here since Daddy died. It's almost like a museum. How about freshening this place up, give it some life! By getting some new curtains and throwing out that old..."

"Charlotte," Amelia rasped sharply, "I'm getting rather tired now." Her voice softened somewhat as she continued, "Why don't you two unpack your things, take a short rest and then go downstairs and have something to eat. Mrs. Mulden has already prepared platters and left them in the refrigerator for you. We'll be able to talk later, when we're all feeling more refreshed." Charlotte left abruptly; walking quickly down the long hall to her old room, she felt perturbed at Amelia's irritability. "I just don't know what will set that woman off," she thought. She unpacked at a furious pace. Rose, leaning over Amelia's bed, kissed her. "Have a good rest dear, we'll see you later." She was relieved to be able to leave her sisters and looked forward to a luxurious nap. She tired easily, the long drive had been fatiguing.

The afternoon sun cast its lengthening shadows over Charlotte and Rose as they sat having lunch at the well-worn kitchen table. Charlotte, still greedily chewing her food, turned her critical eyes on the kitchen. "I see she hasn't gotten rid of a thing down here either. Why, that woman acts as if she hadn't a penny. With all Daddy left, you'd think that..."

"You'd think," Rose snapped, "that you'd have learned by now not raise that subject. You know damn well how Amelia is about Daddy. I don't believe she's ever gotten over his death. Why she's practically appointed herself guardian of his memory. You and I had families to raise, but think how it was for poor Amelia, all alone with nothing but her memories."

"Well it's what she wanted or she wouldn't have done it. She always did exactly what she wanted."

"How can you say that Charlotte!" Rose's voice grew louder, "Amelia was only trying to..." They snapped at each other until Mrs. Mulden hurried into the room to stifle their argument.

"Don't you know we can hear you all the way upstairs? Where's your sense? At a time like this, going at it like a pair of fighting cocks. You know what it does to Miss Amelia when you two fight!" Mrs. Mulden scolded on, "She doesn't have anyone else in the world. I know she's told me dozens of times how she promised her father on his deathbed that she'd take care of you. Why only last night I heard her worrying to herself – 'I must take care of them, I must take care of them.' She kept repeating that. I had a time settling her down for sleep. And now this! You don't make my job any too easy." Charlotte and Rose were silenced.

"I'm sorry," was all that Charlotte could finally think to say. "I don't know why I get so quarrelsome, I'm not usually like this." Rose threw her a sharp look, but Mrs. Mulden's massive presence discouraged any further discord.

"Well," Rose said, trying to smile at Mrs. Mulden, "you're looking quite well, especially considering the strain you've been working under."

"To tell you the truth Miss Rose, I don't feel all that well. As soon as this whole ordeal is over, I'm going to retire and move in with my son and his family. He keeps asking me, you know. I wouldn't have considered it a year ago, but today...I'm just not sure I can face old age alone. But from the way Miss Amelia's been feeling, I don't think my retirement is that far off." A self-conscious silence overcame the three women.

"Well," said Mrs. Mulden forcing them out of the moment, "why don't you two put on some cheerful faces and go up and talk to your sister. I know she's awake-by now ...thanks to you two," she muttered peevishly to herself. Rose and Charlotte stood up and obediently followed Mrs. Mulden's instructions.

"If they aren't like contrite children," Mrs. Mulden mused, as her gaze followed them up the stairs.

"Amelia, are you up?" Rose was tapping gently at her sister's door.

"Of course I am, you can come in now. Did you have a nice lunch?" Her question, aimed at embarrassing her quarrelsome sisters, was cloaked in a honeyed voice. Charlotte and Rose looked at each other sheepishly. Their heads slightly bowed, neither felt entirely prepare for the difficulty of facing Amelia. Amelia smiled at the sight of them so obviously subdued.

"Was that a triumphant smile?" Charlotte wondered to herself as she drew nearer to the bed and sat in the place she had occupied earlier. Rose also seated herself in the chair she had been in that morning.

"Did you have a good lunch?" Amelia inquired again, still smiling. Rose shifted uneasily in her chair.

"Yes, Mrs. Mulden is quite a good cook."

"Oh I know that. She's a rare treasure, that one. I can't think of a sweeter, more devoted person in the world. You can't imagine all the kindness and consideration that she's shown to me during my illness, and it's no small sacrifice on her part. She's no youngster, you know!" Charlotte felt tension constricting her body while Amelia went on talking. She had the disquieting suspicion that Amelia was unfavorably comparing her sisters to Mrs. Mulden. Was Amelia deliberately trying to hurt them?

"I must be overwrought," Charlotte thought trying to rest her fears, "I must be upset over the shrewish way I behave whenever Rose and I get together." Charlotte's conscience chastised her further with the remembrance of her own vicious tongue. It was mainly Charlotte, but Rose too, who could lash out with her hateful words, and wound anyone unfortunate enough to enrage her.

The next few days of the visit were spent trying to avoid any upsetting remarks, but even the most seemingly innocent comment would remind one of the sisters of some past hurt, some bitter half-buried memory. Their being together was an ordeal, just as it always had been. To have it be otherwise would require that the sisters be otherwise.

Charlotte wondered if she were mostly to blame for the rift. She felt a need to love her sisters, for Charlotte's world, though glutted with people, was curiously devoid of any real friendship. She hungered for just one place where she would be welcomed and loved. There were times, only when she had not been in contact with Amelia and Rose for several months, when she felt the rigid knot of hatred loosening its grip, allowing the beginnings of remorse to strain through her. Perhaps she had judged her sisters too harshly. They had all been different people then. If she could forget their past, she could become optimistic about their future.

But the next reunion of the sisters would follow the pattern of the past. It was as though another person lived hidden in the unknown recesses of Charlotte's unconscious. One who listened to her resolutions, remaining dormant until some cue would suddenly waken her, and pushing Charlotte violently aside, burst free. It was then that she found herself losing control, flying into a frenzy, and accusing Rose or Amelia of some past maliciousness. The gap between them grew wider, the edges sharper and more dangerous to bridge.

Though Amelia pretended to be the peacemaker of the family, she too harbored no kindness toward either sister. She would have agreed that Charlotte was the major cause of the rift within the family, but she was not unaware that without Rose's viciously wagging tongue fanning the sparks, their explosive tempers would never have ignited. Amelia had long since controlled her own violent eruptions, cooled slowly over many bleak years. Her once molten anger had hardened like impenetrable lava, encroaching upon the place where her living heart once beat.

She scrutinized her sisters' behavior during the visit, experiencing a cold satisfaction in their continued quarreling. They were proving what no longer needed proving. Amelia's sick, martyred face would stare reproachfully at them. Her expression eloquent — *hateful wretches* — it screamed, while she remained mute.

She continued her reticence while her somber reflection led her back, only half unwillingly, through other days, to yet another battle raging between Charlotte and Rose. Daddy had come home early from his office that still August afternoon. Pale and fatigued, he longed only to free himself of his stifling clothing and to find refuge from the beating sun on the long-shadowed veranda that snaked around the gray stone house.

He sat leaden in his high-backed rocking chair, too exhausted to sip the icy lemonade that Amelia had brought him. The air was becalmed; only the bees hungrily extracting fragrant sweetness from the wilting flowers seemed able to move through the intense heat.

"I did not!" Rose's high-pitched shriek ripped through the stillness like a sudden bolt of jagged lightning.

"You're the only one who knew that I had it, and now it's gone!" Charlotte sobbed.

"What makes you think I'd even want your ridiculous locket?" Their madness persisted.

The weakened man moved heavily in his chair. His hands, groping uncertainly at the sides of the rocker, seemed to search for support. His greyed face strained at the horrible sounds.

"I can never find peace, not even here in my own home," he whispered lifelessly.

"What was that Daddy?" Amelia hovered solicitously over his chair. "Are they bothering you?" She waved her arm angrily in the direction of the voices. "I'll just go and put an end to this!" She turned, about to go into the house, but the distress contorting her father's face stopped her.

"Amelia, you've got to stop those girls, they're going to destroy each other someday. I can't stand much more of it myself. They've got to be stopped," he breathed heavily. "I feel like my chest is caving in. I can't seem to catch my breath in this air."

Amelia stood transfixed, as if she were in a nightmare, helpless to alter the scene playing out before her unwilling eyes. Charlotte and Rose oblivious of everything except their own hostilities kept up their awful screaming.

"They're killing him," Amelia's brain raced wildly, though she was still unable to move. "They're poisoning the air with their venom. That's why Daddy can't breathe, they're killing him..."

He died before the searing light faded from the relentless August sky. The weeks following her father's death were a merciful haze. A high fever and delirium dulled her pain. Lost in fevered sleep, she dreamt that policemen had come, sirens screaming, in a long hearse to take Charlotte and Rose. They were hung for her father's death. When the fever subsided, she awoke to find her sisters standing over her bed. In those first moments of consciousness, she thought that she must have died with them.

"No, you're not dead silly," Rose had smiled at her. "You've just had a very high fever."

Amelia remained confused; the dream had been so real, it was right that her sisters had died. She pulled towards reality. "The wages of sin are...," unable to finish her thought, she sank back into the pillow, exhausted from her effort, she drifted helplessly into sleep. No, time does not heal all wounds. Some can fester an eternity. Some can rupture anew at the slightest provocation, inflicting a fresh agony, a throbbing pain that does not diminish.

During their last hours together, Charlotte labored to bring about conciliation. She wanted desperately for Amelia to feel that there was peace among them, if only to assuage her own guilt. "I was down in the library this morning with Rose, having our coffee, when I saw your portrait. I haven't seen it for years. I can't believe that portrait was painted in 1935 for your eighteenth birthday. I know people always say it seems like yesterday, but it really does. What a beauty you were then, Amelia. That smile...I remember all the young men it dazzled. Why, you were always considered the most beautiful of the Rupert sisters!"

Rose, also eager to make amends and eager not to be cut out of Amelia's will, joined in Charlotte's attempts at making peace. She added to her sister's compliment, "You had so much to smile about then, your youth, your beauty, your always having life your own way..."

"Life my way!" Amelia interrupted irritably. "What makes you think that?" Rose laughed, "Oh come on Amelia, don't get so upset. You know you always could twist anybody to do your bidding... Daddy, all those boyfriends you had."

"If I'm so capable of getting everyone to do my bidding, how is it that I can't get you two to stop your quarreling? No, I haven't gotten my way in everything. But perhaps I still do have something to smile about. I have you two now, don't I?" Her wrinkled hands reached out for theirs and held them for just a moment. She had a surprising grip for one so close to death.

Amelia's eyes suddenly filled with tears, "It's going to be hard to give up everything, to leave my home, and I won't be seeing you again, will I?" Turning her trembling head to gaze at each of her sisters, she sobbed uncontrollably. She was more distraught than either of the women had ever seen her.

Charlotte quickly searched for a handkerchief on Amelia's night table. Her fingers ferreting among the medicines, photographs, and magazines that crowded the small table. She almost toppled over the alarm clock whose relentless ticking had unnerved the sisters during many of their uncomfortable silences. She found a handkerchief and wiped Amelia's pale, hot face. Charlotte spoke soothingly as she dried the streaming tears. "Don't cry, and don't worry about having to give up everything, you never did before. Everything will be fine. We're here now, aren't we? We always will be. There's nothing for you to worry about."

Charlotte's words seemed to have calmed Amelia. She smiled faintly, closed her eyes and slept.

Charlotte and Rose sat in the small hot room listening to the attorney's droning voice mingling with the humid air. It lulled Rose into drowsiness, reminding her of her childhood nap time when alone in her quiet room she would hear the soothing drone of a plane flying high, hidden among the clouds.

"And to Mrs. Mulden, my devoted..." the voice continued. "God!" thought Charlotte, "if you don't listen to the words, it sounds just like the eulogy given at Amelia's funeral. The same modulated voice feigning humility in the presence of death, the same stilted language conveying the same lack of feeling for the deceased."

"And to Charlotte and Rose my dear sisters who..."

Rose startled from her drowsiness, bolted upright in her chair, then leaned forward intent on hearing every word. Charlotte also sat at attention in her place next to Rose. The two women listened in satisfaction as they heard the remainder of Amelia's considerable fortune being divided between them. The only worry that marred the enjoyment of the moment was their concern that they did not appear sufficiently bereft over their recent loss. Both women had involuntarily smiled as they calculated their new riches.

The income from the aforesaid real and personal property is to be distributed annually for a period of ten years in equal shares to my sisters Charlotte and Rose, at the end of the ten-year period all of my property is to be distributed equally to my said sisters. The sole condition to each such distribution is that my sisters Charlotte and Rose shall remain two weeks together in my home with no other person or persons for company. Only after completing the two-week visit are they to receive their annual distribution. This is my final attempt to bring my sisters together.

Rose and Charlotte froze, momentarily stunned at the onerous condition that was placed in the way of their fortune. Rose felt anger and embarrassment that their family quarrels had become public record. She felt apprehension about leaving her own comfortable home to live in what would be an almost certain hell with Charlotte.

Charlotte was frenzied with rage, but struggled to bring herself under control. She wanted nothing to stand in the way of getting her share of the inheritance, not even this! She hated being manipulated, outwitted by Amelia's last will. Her mind raced, thinking of escape, but the living are powerless to change the will of the dead. She was trapped.

"I suggest that you begin the visit as soon as possible." The attorney, sensing resistance from the women, was anxious to avoid any contention that might hinder the dispatch of his duties. He pressed on, "You don't want to delay receiving your inheritance. Would one week from today be mutually agreeable?"

Charlotte and Rose dumbly nodded their acquiescence, neither able to offer any alternative.

The day of the visit dawned gray and sultry. Ominous clouds hung low in the sky. An occasional flash of distant lightning, accompanied by low rumbles of thunder threatened to unleash a furious storm on the defenseless earth. The threat continued on into the day, never materializing, but never ceasing. The oppressive weather unnerved Charlotte and Rose, who were already dreading the prospect of being alone together for two weeks.

"It didn't seem as big to me when I was a little girl," said Rose, forcing herself to make conversation while she walked through the rooms of the old house with Charlotte. "I thought things were supposed to seem larger to you when you're a child."

"I guess all the people filled up the space. Don't forget three children and all the help Daddy had, especially after Mother died, did make a crowd." Charlotte peered in at the familiar rooms trying to recapture the feelings of her youth. Although she was well acquainted with her surroundings, they felt alien to her. A tomb-like quiet filled the rooms. She felt unwelcome here.

The first day of the visit moved with agonizing slowness. Charlotte and Rose tried to avoid each other whenever possible. When it wasn't, they carefully tried to keep their tempers under control by conversing only about what was not preying on their minds.

"The garden looks a little shabby now. I wonder if we should hire a man to keep up the grounds. After all, we will have to be coming back here for the next several years."

"She never gave a damn about the garden before," Charlotte laughed sarcastically to herself. "She only cared about herself, how she looked, and all the men she could get, even if they didn't belong to her. This house could have crashed down around all of us, and as long as it didn't ruffle her hair or soil her dress, she'd have picked her way daintily over the ruins to her next conquest."

"Yes, I suppose it does," was all that Charlotte replied.

"Should we get someone to keep the grounds?" Rose asked again, thinking that parting with some of the inheritance would be torture for Charlotte. She was so miserly! Rose bitterly remembered back to the time when she was first married. She was expecting her daughter then, and David had been out of work. Her father, angry at her elopement, had cut her off. She was destitute. She fought back tears of humiliation as she recalled herself begging, begging her own sister for enough money to live on. Oh God, it was degrading! Charlotte had only laughed, telling her to go out and steal the money, since she never had trouble in taking what didn't belong to her before. Charlotte was still bitterly unforgiving over Rose's marriage to David.

Charlotte who had always loved him, had built her girlhood dreams around that love, but Rose felt no responsibility for Charlotte's loss.

"Maybe David knows someone who could do the job. One of his employees might want some extra work." Rose spoke quietly, never taking her eyes off Charlotte. Charlotte winced at the mention of David's name. Rose could be brutal. She'd feign righteous indignation if anyone accused her of cruelty, but she aimed her barbs with as much skill as a matador poised for the kill, thrusting with the same deadly accuracy.

Charlotte remembered her desolation after David's marriage, but then there was no one to whom she could have spilled out her sorrow. Daddy refused to speak about it – it only reminded him of Rose. All Amelia had been concerned about was not upsetting her father. It was only years later, when Daddy had finally forgiven them, that she could ever speak about her feelings. But by that time she was locked into an unhappy marriage, a pathetic and futile attempt to forget David. "It still hurts," Charlotte almost sobbed aloud.

"Do whatever you want," Charlotte turned, hiding her tears, and hurriedly left the room.

The threat of the approaching storm materialized late that night. The heavy rains continued for days, keeping Charlotte and Rose prisoners inside the walls of the aging house. A heavy shroud of gray clouds pressed against the house, making the world beyond the long windows disappear in the fog. There seemed to be only the house, the two sisters, and their memories. Occasionally the rains would let up and the sunshine, reduced to a feeble yellowish light trying to seep through the overcast sky, would appear. But soon even that faint light would be snuffed out, swallowed by the black storm clouds that swirled above like great birds of prey.

Everything seemed unreal, the hours passed in an eternal monotony. Nothing distinguished one moment from the next. Charlotte often glanced at the clock, but even that seemed unrelated to reality; the revolution of its hands connected to some inner force not intent on marking the time of this world. The hands could have been spinning wildly, or moving as deliberately as death, patiently stalking youth. Its constant measured ticking only reinforced the atmosphere of suspended sameness.

"I can't go on like this," Charlotte moaned softly to herself.

Rose was taciturn and often sat for hours watching the rains turning the earth into mire.

Whenever she caught sight of Charlotte, she'd give her a smug smile, pursing her lips disagreeably. She seemed to enjoy taunting Charlotte with her own loathsome presence.

Rose sat in the library one morning, but this time she was not watching the rains. She had received a letter from her daughter and was eagerly slicing it open.

"We have got to put an end to this madness," Charlotte's harsh voice startled Rose. Charlotte paced the opening of the double doors that led from the hall. She ran her hands distractedly through her disheveled hair. She seemed fatigued, but unable to rest. Rose ignored her with a cold silence, she continued tearing the envelope apart.

"Didn't you hear me?" Charlotte screamed. She was obviously on the verge of losing all control of her violent temper.

"Of course, dear," Rose answered her acidly, "I was just hoping you'd go away."

Charlotte strode into the room. "Well, I'm not going anywhere and neither are you. Jesus Christ, Rose, this whole ordeal is driving me crazy! Why can't we try to reach some sort of accommodation? You must be as upset as I am over the way we've been living. We have to face each other here for another nine years. Can't we make this more bearable?"

"We can only do that if you'd shut up. I was trying to read Marjorie's letter. I just wish for one moment that Amelia could see how disgusting your behavior has been. I'm sure she'd be horrified, and cut you out of her will completely." She glanced up at Amelia's portrait as if she could elicit her approval. "Would you come begging to me for money then, I wonder?" She mused, relishing the scene.

"Oh, you think Amelia had no idea how we'd be during this visit. Well, then you're a bigger fool than I thought possible. She's set us up, dear sister."

"Stop that Charlotte," Rose spoke menacingly to her sister. "Don't say things like that about the dead. I don't like it. All Amelia was trying to do... "

"All Amelia was trying to do!" shrieked Charlotte, "Do you realize how many times we've said those words all through our lives? All Amelia was trying to do was to protect Daddy, all Amelia was trying to do! She's still trying!"

"You're crazy Charlotte! I think you always were. No wonder you never had any kind of marriage. What man could stand you?"

"David." Charlotte stood perfectly still, "Before you came along." Her voice was deadly calm. "If you hadn't gotten pregnant, I doubt if he would have married you." She moved toward Rose, her voice taunting, "Does your daughter know the truth about her pure, sweet mother? Does she Rose? Let's see what you daughter has written to her dearest mother."

Charlotte leaned over her trying to read the letter that Rose now held in back of her. "Is she telling you to bear up, only a few more days with crazy Aunt Charlotte? What lies do you tell her about me?" Trembling, Charlotte ripped the letter out of Rose's hand.

Dear Mother,

I hope that you're keeping up your spirits under the circumstances you're living under. Cheer up... only one more week to go. I do have some news, though, that might do just that. I was going through some of the old furniture in the attic, you know how I get on rainy days with nothing to do. Well, guess what I found hidden behind a lot of your old mementos – a beautiful locket. ALWAYS DAVID is engraved on the back. I know you'll be happy to wear it again. You're so sentimental about anything that Daddy's ever given you. We're looking forward to seeing you very soon.

Love,

Marjorie

"Oh-God-Oh! My locket!" A cry of anguish tore from Charlotte's throat. She crumpled the letter still in her grasp, and ripped it apart, hurling its fragmented remains at Rose. Suddenly Charlotte grew calmer, her cries ceased. A merciless grin twisted her mouth. "Maybe it's time that I took something away from you. I can finally do that now. I think that Marjorie should know everything about you."

Rose's face twisted with pain. "You'd better leave her out of this," she threatened. Charlotte's mocking face pushed closer. "Will you tell her Rose, or should I?"

"Shut up! Shut up!" she shrilled. She lunged at Charlotte, obsessed with driving that hideously sardonic grin from her face. Her hands sprung at Charlotte's throat. Charlotte cringed with loathing at the touch of her despised sister. All the hatred she had nurtured within her burst like an abscess at that touch. Its venom destroyed her reason. She began savagely pounding Rose into submission. With each blow she tried to make her feel all the pain she had ever suffered.

Rose struggled against this furious assault, but, exhausted, lost her balance and stumbled, falling backwards. She felt a sharp crack at the back of her head, she was dazed, the room grew dimmer. "If I can just reach... " Her long arm strained towards the letter opener still lying on the sofa.

Their bodies were found several days later, lying twisted in a macabre embrace, beneath the vacant stare and frozen smile of the young Amelia.

TAPESTRY

PART ONE

Does the insect know, when it steps lightly on the first silken strand of the spider's web, what the future holds?

The slamming of the back door startled Karen. She quickly dropped her book and turned towards the sudden sound.

"It's me Mom," shouted Lori.

"Oh, I just sat down and started reading a new book. I've been hearing so much about it, I thought I'd see what all the fuss was about."

"What book?"

"The Woven Web."

"Sorry I interrupted, but I wanted to talk to you about a few things, and see how you're doing."

Karen smiled and kissed Lori, her only child, who'd grown into a beautiful and competent woman.

"Now that you're here, I'm fine."

"That's not the answer I was hoping for, and it's why I came over."

"Are you ok?"

"I'm great, it's you I'm concerned about. I think it's time we had a talk."

"Uh, oh, I'm not in trouble am I?" teased Karen. It had been a family joke. Anytime her parents wanted to "have a talk", Lori knew she was in trouble. Even though it had been years ago, they both still laughed about it. But Lori wasn't laughing now.

"Well, in a way, I think you are in trouble. Daddy's heart attack was almost two years ago and since he's been gone I don't see you really getting on with your life."

"I don't know about that. I started reading the book so I could talk to the people at the library about it, you know to be part of the group."

"Volunteering to read to kids once a week and having a little conversation with the other volunteers hardly makes a life."

"What would you have me do, become an explorer?" She wanted to keep the conversation from getting serious. Lori would not cooperate.

"I'm serious, you wanted to travel for years, and Daddy always said 'next year.' That was his motto. Mom, there is no 'next year.' Only you can make it 'this year.' You always put him and me ahead of yourself. There's no purpose to that anymore. Daddy's gone, and the sale of his business left you and me with enough money to last both our lifetimes. You have no responsibilities. You're overdue to start having the fun you deserve, while you're still young enough to enjoy life. At fifty-two, you could have forty years left. You know how long people live in your family. It's time to get out and take a starring role in your own life."

Karen's eyes filled with tears. She blinked them back and turned her head to hide from Lori's insistent gaze. Lori was right, of course, but the truth she hid, even from herself for so many years, was that she had become afraid to leave her familiar comfortable surroundings. She was terrified of the unknown.

"Listen", Lori persisted, "Nick and I think you should go to London. You remember how much fun he and I had there last year. It'll be an easy trip. No language problems, lots to do and see. We loved it!"

"Of course you did, sweetie, you were there with your husband."

"Yes, but you could still have an incredible time on your own. We want to give that trip to you as a gift. We also want to give you this." She reached into her pocket, removed a small velvet box, and handed it to her mother. Inside was a beautiful diamond star shaped pendant.

"Wearing it will remind you to be the star of your own life. It'll bring you luck."

"Good or bad?" quipped Karen.

Lori's face voiced her disapproval.

"I know, no negativity."

Karen's tears fell freely, but now they weren't all from fear.

"Can I say no?"

"No!" Lori shot back.

Karen hesitated, thinking of her therapist's advice. The grief counselor she went to after Andy's death recommended a psychologist, Dr. Salwyn, who was also urging her to travel.

"It's not a lifetime commitment. What have you got to lose?" She could still hear him saying that now.

Karen relented, "ok, ok, I give up. You win."

"No, Mom, hopefully you win."

Karen wouldn't have had the courage to agree without Dr. Salwyn's help. He had gently guided her to open the door to her past. "It will only help you make better choices in the future."

In their sessions he encouraged her to talk, and at last, someone listened.

She couldn't tell when she had changed from a young bride, eager to experience a life of love and adventure, into the woman she had become.

When they were first married there was no money to go anywhere. Besides, whatever little they had, Andy saved to start his business. Then she became pregnant with Lori. Andy begged her to quit teaching to take care of their baby. "I can take care of the both of you now", he said. His idea of taking care of them was to spend more and more time working.

"I want you and Lori to have everything."

"When I married you," she cried, "you were everything I wanted."

"Do we have to go there again? You know a business doesn't run by itself."

Neither does a marriage, she thought, but gave up trying to change him. His response would have been more extravagant gifts for her and Lori. She wondered if what he really enjoyed was showing off the proof of his success. When she'd dress to go out, wearing a new outfit or piece of jewelry, he'd say, "That looks great, Karen." Never, "You look great, Karen".

Cats bring their owners dead mice to show off their hunting skills. Karen got dead minks to wear to show off Andy's.

People gravitated towards her charismatic husband. "You're so lucky to be married to Andy", they'd say to her, and turn their attention back to him. She stopped trying to engage anyone when he was around. It became easier to find comfort in her familiar routine, living in her beautiful home, raising Lori. She didn't want the world to reach in and hurt her. Out there she was a reflection of his success. But even in here, as she looked in the mirror, she felt she was just a reflection of herself.

Dr. Salwyn and Lori had convinced her it was time to start a new chapter in her life.

Karen sipped her second cup of coffee slowly, reluctant to leave the cheerful hotel restaurant. The lunch crowd was mostly gone, leaving the room empty, except for her and one other person. This was the afternoon of her third day in London and she was already regretting her decision to come. She had gone on a tour yesterday and had no particular schedule for the rest of the day. The view of London from the tour bus was overwhelming. The streets were a confusing labyrinth, many were centuries old. Often modern life was set on ancient bones. The noise and exhaust competed for spaces clogged by traffic and pedestrians. How could she possibly find her way on her own? She was trying to be fearless, and it wasn't working out as she had hoped.

The waiters were too polite to rush her, but she sensed they were anxious for her to leave. But as soon as she'd leave, she faced an empty afternoon and an equally empty life. The other diner, a distinguished looking man about her age, also appeared to be in no hurry to finish his cup of tea or his newspaper. That gave her the courage to linger a bit longer. She glanced over at him, planning to leave when he did. He put his paper aside and turned in her direction. A look of shock momentarily flashed across his face. He regained his composure, but now was staring at her. She couldn't believe such an attractive man was looking at her like that, but it was not her imagination.

Why had she attracted his interest? She never dressed for attention, preferring simple understated clothing. It would require an educated eye to realize she had an expensive wardrobe. Today she had added the diamond star.

Karen finally put down her cup and signaled for the waiter. The staring man, as she had nicknamed him, abruptly got up and approached her table. Handing his credit card to the waiter, he said "This lady is my guest, please put it on my card."

Karen involuntarily clutched her star.

"Oh that's not necessary," she burst out, but the waiter was already hurrying to do as the stranger had ordered.

"I hope you don't think me too forward, but when I saw you I said to myself, who is that terribly attractive woman? I must meet her. Please allow me to introduce myself, Nigel Craxford."

She offered her hand, which he took in both of his, accompanied by a warm disarming smile.

"Karen Miller", she managed.

"I'm not going to pretend I haven't been staring at you. It's not only that I find you terribly attractive, but I also thought we might have met before."

"Maybe I just have a common face."

"There's nothing common about you."

"Unless you've been to Allentown, Pennsylvania, not exactly a tourist hotspot, we haven't met. I must remind you of someone else you've met, somewhere else in your past."

"Well, I'm not really so interested in the past, rather the future. Do you have any plans for the rest of the afternoon?"

Oh God, Karen thought, this can't be happening to me, especially at my age. As usual, Karen underestimated herself. Years of neglect had made her unaware of her quiet beauty.

"Not really," she said, amazed that she was able to answer in a normal voice. Her mind was racing, her heart pounding.

"I'm here on business, by myself. I live in a little village, Shincliffe, right outside Durham. It's north of here. Anyway, I thought since I love London, I'd come a few days early and treat myself to a holiday. There are a lot of places, walking distance from here, that you might find interesting. And I know I'm interested in getting to know you. So what do you say to both of us taking a chance? How risky can that be?"

She hesitated, but realized it would be a great story to tell when she got home.

"Why not?"

They stepped out into a heavy rain. Yesterday had also been rainy. Low dark clouds hovered over the city, depressing Karen. She'd felt lonely and anxious. The weather hadn't changed, but with Nigel at her side, she had. They had to lean in close together to avoid being soaked. She felt an instant connection to him as he protected her from the downpour. She who was normally so reticent, was amazed at how easy conversation was with him. They spent the next few hours talking and laughing.

As they left the last museum the city was dark. Fog surrounded them. Sheltered under his umbrella, she couldn't see the world beyond him. Now arm in arm in comfortable silence, they walked for several blocks until they came to an inviting looking pub. Flower filled window boxes flanked the entrance. Soft light spilled from the windows and shone on the raindrops clinging to the petals. She hadn't noticed any flowers yesterday. They looked at each other, smiled and went in for dinner.

They settled at their table, happy to be out of the weather. Shadows from flickering candles moved across the whitewashed walls and low beamed ceiling. The cozy room, a respite from the frantic pace of the city. The waiter approached for their order.

"I'll have a pint of Guinness and a shandy for my lady".

Hearing that upper class British accent, she could imagine him a knight and she his lady. Stop being ridiculous, she told herself. She felt like a foolish young girl. But in spite of her age, the foolish young girl had a will to live. She was surprised how much she enjoyed her shandy. She had never cared for beer or ginger ale, and yet the odd combination was delicious. She thought she and Nigel an odd combination, but perhaps they'd also be wonderful together. It was during dinner that he complimented her on her star.

"It does suit you, bright and beautiful. I'll have to call you Star."

"Karen will do." Though secretly she preferred Star.

When Karen woke the next morning, she was not alone. Doubt had rejoined her and was now in control of her thoughts. She relived the moments she had spent with Nigel and refused to believe he could actually be attracted to her. When he said goodnight, it was with a light kiss on each cheek. His last words were "I'll call." That's how you could say goodnight to your grandmother. And wasn't "I'll call" a polite way of saying you'll never hear from me again? She felt a complete fool to be so enamored with a man she barely knew.

The phone ringing by her bed interrupted the fresh round of attacks she was planning to launch against herself.

"Good morning Star. Did you have a good night?"

Karen could have cried with relief at the sound of Nigel's voice.

"Yes I did. The room is very comfortable and quiet."

"Good, then perhaps you'll be ready for more sightseeing today. The weather has cleared and I have lots of plans for you."

"I'm all yours."

"That's exactly what I hoped you'd say."

Their day together was wonderful. Feeling relaxed by Nigel's attention, her anxiety and doubt ebbed away. When she spoke, he listened to her the way Dr. Salwyn did, and she had to pay for that.

The following day they spent antiquing. He guided her through a maze of winding streets and alleys, finding obscure shops. He had an instinct for quality and frequently discovered overlooked treasures. He was eager to share his knowledge, and warned her, "It's not always easy to spot a fake."

The first time Nigel kissed her, really kissed her, happened early one evening as they stood in Greenwich Park overlooking the Thames. She had been going on about something she found particularly amusing. These last few days she found so much to be amused about. What a chatterbox she had become, now that she had an interested audience. Nigel, however, seemed not to be listening to her story. He leaned down toward her and whispered, "If you'll stop talking for a moment I'll kiss you." With that, he tipped her face towards his, took her in his arms and kept his promise.

Karen stayed in his arms.

"You're making it so hard for me to leave."

"That's the plan."

He took her back to her hotel. This time she had no doubt about his feelings. Eager to be alone, they walked quickly through the opulent lobby. Nigel made no comment when she opened the door to her luxurious suite. Driven by desire, he came to her, not as a stranger, but as a lover who knew how to arouse all her passions. He undressed her slowly, caressing and admiring each part of her body. "You are a star," he murmured hoarsely, "the most beautiful heaven ever made." She stopped his words with her mouth, kissing him deeply, trying to find his soul. Her world disappeared in his embrace. All she could feel was what he was doing to her body.

Morning brought the most contentment and calm that Karen had ever known. She saw his still sleeping face and stared at the man who had brought her such pleasure during the night. It didn't seem possible that they had met only a week ago. He turned towards her as he woke, reaching for her before he spoke. When he did speak, she couldn't believe his words.

"Marry me."

"What?"

"Marry me," he repeated.

"We hardly know each other."

He turned onto his back, stretching out his lean body, he rested his hands behind his head and looked away from her. He directed his gaze at the ceiling for a few silent moments. He seemed upset, disappointed.

"Well here's something you can know about me. Love at first sight, runs in my family. My parents became engaged five weeks after they met, and were married for forty-six years. With you I feel complete. It's like I've lost something and found it again in you."

Karen regained enough control of her emotions to answer sensibly. "We still don't know enough about each other yet."

"I know what I feel."

"I know what I feel too, but that's no reason to rush."

"No reason to rush, what about your trip here coming to an end? You're supposed to go back home next weekend."

"I can postpone that. I'll see if I can make some arrangement with the hotel to extend my stay. I'll email Lori to let her know I'm changing my return date."

That's all she was willing to let Lori know now. If this all ended badly, there was no way she wanted to face what she knew would be a lengthy interrogation. Some things are best kept secret.

Karen was now engulfed in confusion. She was no longer able to hold her emotions in check. Having broken free, they scattered in all directions, leaving her hopelessly at sea. Clearly she was smitten with Nigel, probably even in love. She had longed for Andy to be much more of a husband and a lover, and now when she was so passionately pursued, she felt guilty. Like she was cheating. A lot of the guilt was there because she knew how much she wanted Nigel. Was she shallow and disloyal falling so easily into the arms of someone new? Nigel studied her face and sensed her torment. "Karen," he said gently, "the last thing I wanted to do was to upset you. Think about us, and what we could have together. I need time to rearrange my schedule too, so I can stay on longer. Perhaps I should do all that tomorrow. That would give you a day on you own, without any pressure, so you can sort out what you need to. I'll call you the day after. If you need more time, don't worry, I'll be here whenever you want me." She nodded mutely in agreement.

Nigel left the hotel confident he would not lose Karen. Understanding her reservations, he would do nothing to frighten her away. You don't come across a woman like her often. Instinct told him she was a prize worth having. He knew he could win her trust, it just required patience and skill. Years by the water had made him an excellent fisherman.

The day without him felt all wrong, but her time alone enabled her to realize that she did not want to spend the remainder of her life alone without love. She was able to put Andy to rest and say her final goodbye to her marriage. She knew Andy had said his goodbye to their marriage years before he died. She was ready to face the future without burdens from the past.

Nigel, careful of her feelings, didn't put any pressure on her to reach a decision. His mood was lighthearted and playful. He brought a camera along and announced that they were going to have an outing to Oxford. "I've hired a car for the day, we can be back here after dinner."

They made their way through the winding streets of the beautiful old city. Oxford, the city of spires, with its pealing bells and many steeples all vying for heaven's attention. He stopped her several times to pose in front of places that were particularly picturesque. They did not speak of tomorrow, only today. For lunch he had managed to pick up a hamper at Taylors, a restaurant that specialized in providing gourmet picnics. He went back to the car to retrieve an oilcloth and a blanket to put over it. Karen looked at him, "You think of everything."

"I try."

Their destination was the Rainbow Bridge on the River Cherwell, a favorite picnic spot for locals and tourists. It was a rare English summer day. It had rained during the night. The day, freshly washed, sparkled in the sun. They spread out their picnic under a tree that hung over the river. A fresh breeze rustled the branches, releasing a sudden shower of raindrops that had remained on the leaves. They laughed in surprise, their picnic dampened, but not their spirits. Karen bloomed in the soft summer day. Her blue eyes sparkled, her cheeks grew rosy.

Nigel took out his camera again and took several more photographs of her. "I'm really trying to capture you." At last he seemed satisfied. "I'll show you these, when they're developed. I hope you like them." She was impressed that he didn't use a cell phone for a camera. He seemed knowledgeable about photography.

They left rather late, tired from their long day. As Nigel drove them back to London, she rested her head on his shoulder and snuggled against his arm. She couldn't wait to fall into bed, but this time it was only sleep she longed for. She was almost giddy with exhaustion. "I have to warn you," she giggled, "my family lives forever, so if I do say yes, you could be stuck with me for a long time."

Nigel kept his eyes on the dark road ahead of them.

"I'm not worried."

Karen stepped hurriedly out of the shower and glanced at the small clock on her dressing table. It was a gift from Nigel. When he gave it to her, smiling mischievously, he told her "Whenever you look at it, you have to think it's time for Nigel." She couldn't help but be charmed and flattered. But looking at the clock now, she realized time was running out. There was a lot she needed to do before Nigel came for her. He was taking her to dinner at Rules, a famous old restaurant in Covent Garden and then to the theater. She wanted to look her best. Sitting down in front of her mirror, she was pleased with what she saw. Gone was the timid mouse afraid of the world. Now she saw not just a reflection, but herself, vibrant, confident and pretty. She had blossomed. New growth flowered on an old branch.

She loved Rules, dark and clubby, walls crowded with pictures. It was perfect. Her eyes darted around the room, trying to take it all in.

"I'm over here." Nigel joked, bringing her attention back to him.

"Oh, I'm sorry." Karen stammered, embarrassed that that she appeared rude.

"I'm kidding." Nigel reassured her. "It's just the reaction I wanted you to have, as well as this." He handed her a small shopping bag she hadn't noticed before. She reached in and pulled out a beautiful scarf. The design was a copy of an Audubon print, a pair of bluebirds perched on a flowering branch. It too was perfect.

"I thought the blue would be just the thing for your eyes. Let's see how it looks." He placed the scarf lightly around her neck. She loved its silken feel.

The play, a hit in London and New York, was wonderful. The only problem was the audience laughed so long, she occasionally missed hearing some lines. How long can this fairytale life go on, she wondered?

She still hid the truth from Lori, telling her only, as Lori already suspected, that she had met someone. She assured her she was having fun, but it was nothing serious. She spoke to her daughter frequently and sounded so happy that Lori was convinced that something more serious was going on, but respected her mother's privacy. After all, it had been her idea for Karen to go.

Nigel thought perhaps, it was time to propose again. Again the answer was no. Now she was sure that she loved him and told him that, but something in her still hesitated. He understood her feelings, but insisted they were destined for each other.

"Ever since we first met, I felt I knew you and that we belonged together. So for me, I don't think it's too soon, but overdue. I'm not discouraged, I'm optimistic that soon you'll agree."

Since they had been in London for several weeks now, Nigel explained that he had business to deal with that required some occasional meetings here in London and also some travel. During the times she was on her own, he was never far from her heart. She delighted in spending that time shopping for things she knew he would enjoy, handcrafted chocolates, a favorite wine or clothing she thought he'd look good in. She never discussed her financial situation with him, but knew it was evident from her ability to extend her stay and remain in her suite that she was quite affluent. But aside from the small gifts that he happily accepted, he never allowed her to pay for anything. He insisted it was his job to take care of her. It was reassuring that he didn't appear to be interested in her money. In fact, it was he who was trying to convince her that he was able to provide for all her needs.

Apparently he had run a successful import-export business that had taken him to all parts of the world. He told her he was in the process of finalizing a deal to sell the business. He was looking forward to retirement. In addition to that, he had inherited quite a bit from his mother's side of the family, including a small cottage in Cornwall. It had been in his mother's family for generations and meant a great deal to him. "I'll have to take you there. I'm not telling you all this to boast, but to show you that when, not if, you say yes, you'll know you're not marrying a pauper."

"I didn't think you were."

Shortly after that conversation, he told her he had just heard from his cousin Amanda, who had moved to Australia with her family when Nigel was still an infant. The families had remained in touch, in spite of the distance. Now her mother, his mother's sister, had died and wanted Nigel to have a few antiques that had been in the family for as long as anyone could remember. She was shipping them by freighter, so didn't know exactly when they'd arrive. "I'm guessing that's the last of my inheritance."

It took Nigel somewhat longer to discuss a painful part of his past. He asked to go to her suite so they could speak in private. She had confessed to him that she had had a lonely marriage with Andy. She knew he had been married also and that his wife had died, but he had given no further details, and had quickly changed the subject. She didn't press him, assuming he'd talk about it when he was ready. This was exactly the kind of thing she felt it was important to know before making any commitment to him. He never talked about his late wife. Now she would learn why.

"Susan and I married young and were very much in love. We then had a beautiful daughter, Pamela. Our lives were perfect. We were on holiday in Italy, just after Pam's fourth birthday, when a drunk driver came out of nowhere and killed Susan instantly. Pam lingered for another day. I was behind the wheel, knocked unconscious. I never saw who did it. The car sped away before I ever knew what happened. They were killed while I was driving. I recovered from the accident, but not from their deaths. I can't forgive myself for what happened. I was supposed to protect my family, instead I lost them! I'm an only child, so aside from my cousin in Australia, I have no family. Of course, there are friends, but that's not the same. I threw myself into my work, travelling around the world. You can't put down roots that way, which is exactly what I wanted. I couldn't bear to risk such heartbreak again. I was too cowardly. Their faces haunted me. I even burned their photographs. There are no traces left of them in my life. I wasn't willing to take another chance on love, until I met you."

Nigel finished his story. He hung his head down, looking at the floor, and was silent. He appeared utterly defeated. "Finally telling this story makes me want to cry, but it's not easy for a man to cry." Karen, who had been sitting in a chair next to his, jumped up and gathered him in her arms. "It wasn't your fault. You poor man. You have nothing to feel guilty about. Another person came out of nowhere and destroyed your life. How could you even begin to think you were in anyway responsible for anything so cruel? What could you have done to prevent that? Nothing!"

He was more subdued than usual for a couple of days afterwards, but soon his spirits lifted, and was again cheerfully making plans for the two of them. She was grateful for that. She wondered if Nigel could be suffering from post-traumatic stress as a result of the accident. She saw no signs of it, but also saw no reason not to proceed with caution.

On their next outing, Nigel hired a convertible sports car, perfect he said, for touring the countryside. Karen had seen pictures, of course, but nothing could compare to actually driving the narrow winding roads through storybook villages. The gently rolling scenery stretched out on either side of the road. She had never seen so many beautiful shades of green. Nigel declared that God had created the English countryside so that He would have somewhere to go on holiday. Karen was inclined to agree with him.

Karen saw no evidence of trauma from Nigel's past. Being home again seemed to heal him. She loved the land almost as much as he did, but for her it still wasn't home. As wonderful as her life had become, it was increasingly difficult to be away from her daughter. Each time she got off the phone with Lori she suffered pangs of homesickness. She could only imagine how much worse it will be when Lori and Nick have children. Since Lori had gotten married she looked forward to becoming a grandmother. She never questioned them about when they were going to start a family, but everyone knew how much she loved holding a baby in her arms. Lori even asked if Karen would pay any attention to her, once a baby arrived. Of course she wasn't serious, knowing how much she was loved by her mother.

Karen hovered between two worlds. Should she remain in hers or be taken into Nigel's? She couldn't live in both.

Torn between her growing love for Nigel and her longing to be at home with her daughter, was becoming increasingly difficult. Nigel wanted them to live in England and travel to Allentown for visits. Knowing his background, she didn't want to cause him any more grief. To tear him away from his roots just as he was finding happiness again was unthinkable. But she had roots too, and wasn't sure she could live on foreign soil.

While she was in this state of mind, it appeared that fate had already decided for her. She hardly recognized Nigel's barely audible voice, when he called her early one morning. She was dreaming that the phone was ringing, it grew so loud it woke her up. It was her phone that was ringing.

"I have to see you."

"What?" She tried to focus.

"I have to see you now." His voice grew louder.

"I was sleeping, you woke me up."

"I'm coming right over, get out of bed."

He had rented a small flat near her hotel. She had found it charmingly old fashioned that he would not live together until they were married.

He was at her door within twenty minutes. In the time it took him to arrive, she had frantically run through every possible disastrous scenario she could imagine. Had his old fears returned, making him unwilling to have a relationship? Was he suffering mood swings as a result of the horrific accident? Was he diagnosed with a terrible, possibly fatal disease? Or, perhaps, he realized he just didn't love her, and his conscience couldn't be clear until he told her face to face, that it was over. She prepared herself for every dream to be destroyed when he arrived. But there was no way she could have prepared herself for what occurred.

Nigel entered the suite, walked past her and placed a large package on a desk in the sitting room. He looked like he hadn't slept. Without any introduction he immediately blurted out his tale. "I got word yesterday afternoon that the shipment from Australia had arrived. By the time I could get to pick it up, it was the end of the day. I had that business dinner I told you about last night. I wanted to go over some paperwork beforehand and so took the box from the shipping office back to my flat. It wasn't overly large or heavy, and frankly I really wasn't very curious about what was in it. I got back late from dinner and then decided I might as well open the box. It contained a few silver serving pieces, candlesticks, a small oil painting and this package." Opening the package as he was speaking, he went through many layers of tissue paper before he removed an ancient looking tapestry. He stopped talking, removed the tapestry and held it up for her to see.

Karen gasped at the sight. The tapestry was badly worn, but it was easy to see what it depicted. There against a highly stylized floral background was a couple in medieval clothing. The man looked like Nigel, the woman looked like her! Karen felt as if she had received a heavy blow to her heart, she was short of breath and couldn't speak. She looked to Nigel, then back at the tapestry. He said nothing.

"Yes" was all she finally said.

Karen's days were spent in happy preparation for her marriage. She decided not to tell Lori since they planned to be married privately, and to make a trip to Allentown shortly after the honeymoon. It would not be very long now. She was imagining how exciting it was going to be, arriving at the airport with her handsome new husband. When she was home again, they would celebrate with Lori and Nick. She couldn't wait to share her news and tell the amazing story of their courtship. Nigel loved telling her that he had been right about them all along. "Our lives are woven together. That should be our family motto."

One evening, only a few weeks before their wedding, Nigel broached the subject of a will.

"Listen," he said, "You aren't automatically entitled to inherit from me if I die. In the UK, you have to draw up a will if you want your spouse to inherit your money. So what I want to do, is take you to my solicitor and have him put you in my will. I want you to get everything in case anything should happen to me."

Karen hated the idea of even discussing the possibility that she could lose him. "Let's be practical, I'm in good health and I don't think anything will happen for a very long time. But just in case it did, I need to know you'll be well taken care of, by me."

"Nigel, you know I'm a wealthy woman. I'm very touched that you want to do this, but I've actually been frustrated that you've never let me do much for you. I really don't need anything from you."

"That may be the case, but I need something from you. After what happened to Susan and Pam, I have to feel I'm protecting you. You don't know what it's like for a man not to be able to care for his family. It's devastating. I have to know that no matter what, even after death, I'm providing for you. You could give it all away, if you want, but I need you to have this. Please Karen, give me this and I won't ask another thing of you."

Karen agreed, on one condition. "Then I have to leave everything to you. Except for some charities that are important to me, and the jewelry and a few personal items that I want Lori to have, everything else is for you."

"Absolutely not! That's not what I want or need. Don't you want Lori to have everything? She's going to have a family someday. It costs a lot of money to raise children."

"Andy left her so much, she and Nick couldn't spend it in a lifetime. Besides, both of them have very successful careers. I told you that she was a lawyer, and Nick was a real estate developer. What I didn't tell you is that they make so much, and have inherited so much, that they give large amounts away every year. So they certainly don't need a thing."

Nigel reluctantly agreed and made an appointment with his solicitor.

A pleasant middle-aged receptionist ushered them into Simon Blair's handsomely furnished office. Simon was well passed middle age. He was a portly, balding man with a kindly face, and an excellent reputation. Karen felt they were in good hands. "Come in, come in." Simon welcomed them and urged them to sit down. The receptionist followed and offered tea.

"I understand that congratulations are in order. I wish you both a long and happy marriage."

Nigel told Simon what he wanted. Then Simon turned to Karen, as she told him what she wanted, Nigel again objected. "Simon, it's not what I want. Can't you talk her out of it?"

Karen would not be dissuaded. The solicitor laughed, "I've seen couples argue before, but never over anything like this. It's a first. If that's all you ever disagree about, I predict that you will have a long, happy marriage I know you are anxious to have this wrapped up as soon as possible. We'll get to it straight away. Again, my best wishes to you both."

After they left the office, Nigel turned to Karen. "I haven't been completely honest with you."

"In what way?"

"There is one thing more I want you to do. Don't look so suspicious, hear me out. I've made reservations for you at The Grove. It's a beautiful spa resort not too far from London. You should have some days of complete pampering before our wedding. The next few days will be filled with all sorts of odds and ends that need my attention. I'll feel much happier if I know you're safely tucked away in such a wonderful place."

Karen shook her head in disbelief. "I don't deserve you."

Karen rose early. While dew still covered the grass, she went outside to breath the fresh scent of morning. The other guests were still asleep. Karen walked the expansive grounds of the hotel, alone in her paradise.

At breakfast she was looking at the schedule for the day's activities, trying to decide what class she wanted to attend after her hot stone massage. A woman at the adjoining table was lecturing her friend on the benefits of yoga.

"Excuse me," Karen interjected herself into the conversation. "I couldn't help overhearing your conversation about yoga. I was thinking of trying it."

The woman, happy to give her opinion to yet another person, went on at length about all its benefits.

"Well, thank you. I'm convinced."

The woman smiled broadly, pleased to have made a new convert. At the end of the class, Karen felt calm, yet energized. She was glad she had tried it. She approached the instructor, introduced herself, and let her know how much she enjoyed the class. "I'm getting married soon, and moving to Shincliffe. Do you happen to know any place there I could take classes? Or anybody that you could personally recommend who teaches yoga?"

"Thank you, it's always nice to hear from my students about liking the practice of yoga. I don't know anything about Shincliffe. I only know of some places in Durham, which is close by, but you're in luck. Emily Wadhams, who manages the spa, is from Shincliffe, I'll take you to her.

She took her to a small office right off the spa reception area and introduced her.

"Emily, this is... " Karen, realizing the instructor had forgotten her name, came to her rescue.

"Karen Miller," she said extending her hand. The instructor gave her a grateful look.

Emily and Karen spoke for a while. Then Karen asked if she knew Nigel.

"Nigel Craxford, that name doesn't sound familiar. It's a small place, I know most of the people, but I moved here almost two years ago, so he could have come after I left."

She gave Karen the name of a studio that she liked, and wished her good luck in her new life. At the end of the day, Emily realized she could call her sister Penny, who still lived in Shincliffe. Penny was an estate agent and would know, not only if there were any new yoga studios, but could also look up the real estate records for any property purchased by a Nigel Craxford. She thought Karen would like that.

When she reached Penny, her sister mentioned the same yoga studio that Emily had already told Karen about, but she wasn't able to find any record of any home purchases made by Nigel Craxford, at least not in the past seven years. Emily looked for Karen to tell her, but was too late, she was already gone.

Nigel spent the time away from Karen taking care of what he needed to do with before going on the honeymoon.

On the last day before Karen was due back, Nigel wrapped up his final piece of business. It was almost one o'clock, and Nigel was ravenous. He went to his favorite restaurant, the same place he had met Karen. It was expensive, but the food was excellent. It was very popular with the ladies who lunch.....alone.

One of the things he told Karen he wanted to do was to get the tapestry restored.

"It's going to hang in a special place in our home, and right now it's in no condition for that. Besides, I don't want it to deteriorate."

"Do you think it's valuable?" she asked.

"Priceless." he replied.

After lunch Nigel took a cab to Winkley Street. It was a mix of commercial buildings and renovated lofts. Some of them had been made into very attractive apartments. He stopped in front of Beasley's Antiques.

The sign outside read 'Antiques, Repairs, and Restorations. Fine Weaving Done on Premises'. Mr. Beasley was sitting behind the counter of his dark cluttered shop, and saw Nigel as he entered.

"Hello sir, good to see you again. How are you?"

Nigel didn't answer, He dropped a package on the counter and pushed a photograph towards Mr. Beasley.

It was of a woman, neither young, nor old, nor especially pretty. Her trusting brown eyes were her best feature.

"Same thing as usual?" Beasley questioned.

"Yes."

"Mr. Beasley opened the package and examined the contents. The tapestry is getting pretty worn. I'll have to make a few extra repairs this time."

"No problem."

Lori sat the dinner table toying with her food. She had no appetite. Besides the nausea that had been plaguing her recently, she felt anxious.

"I'm just not comfortable with Mom's being away so long. Nick, you know it's not like her. I don't have a good feeling about what's going on over there. As soon as I get this stomach problem resolved, I'm going over there," she announced.

"You said yourself she sounds happy. Don't you think you're overreacting?"

Those words did not sit well with Lori, she shot him a sharp look. She hated when he accused her of that.

"You never think anything could be wrong. I think sometimes you can be naïve."

"I'll admit to that. But your mother is a grown woman, and a smart one at that. Give her some credit. She wasn't born yesterday."

"Yeah, but she doesn't have a lot of experience with men. Daddy was her first boyfriend. I don't want her going all overboard on some gigolo just because he's paying attention to her."

"Oh, she doesn't have the experience you have, international woman of the world. I mustn't forget that you dated that Danish foreign exchange student back in high school."

Lori swiped him with her napkin and laughed. She found it impossible to stay mad at him.

Lori rushed to meet Nick at the front door as soon as she heard him coming home. She didn't even greet him, but started right in. "It looks like this stomach thing isn't going to go away anytime soon."

"What's wrong?" He looked worried.

"Well, the doctor said... " another wave of nausea hit Lori before she could finish. Nick followed her anxiously to the bathroom. When she finally stopped retching, she continued. "I'M PREGNANT! WE'RE HAVING A BABY!" She grabbed Nick's hands and started to jump up and down. "The only downside is I don't know when I'll be able to go to London. The doctor said some people can have severe nausea for a while. It usually resolves in a few weeks, but it could take even longer. She wants to keep an eye on things to make sure I don't get dehydrated. Dr. Gerber said it's nothing to worry about, as long as I'm monitored. There are medications, but she's conservative and prefers I don't take anything unless it's absolutely necessary. She's very optimistic and said everything looks normal. I'm not going to tell Mom anything now. I'll wait until I go over there and give her the news in person. It'll have to keep til then."

Nigel had suggested they honeymoon at his cottage in Cornwall, in the village of Mousehole.

"Mousehole," she questioned incredulously, "who would name a place Mousehole?"

"Englishmen."

"And who would honeymoon in a place called Mousehole?"

"Dylan Thomas."

"What am I getting into?" she laughed. "Well, I had to be persuaded to come to London, and look how that turned out. So I guess I should give Mousehole a chance." She continued laughing.

Once it was decided, Nigel became very excited. He was absent from London again, for days at a time. "I have a lot to do before we go." He would not share any details. He suggested that they take the scenic route. "It's almost a six-hour drive. If we go the scenic way, it will be a lot longer, but I think it's worth it. There are some lovely old towns along the way. If we get impatient we can always hop back on the motorway. The only disadvantage is that we'll reach Mousehole at night. You'll have to wait for morning to really see it."

"As long as I'm with you."

The sun did not shine on the bride and groom. A misty drizzle blanketed the city. The bridal bouquet of fresh flowers, so recently plucked from life at their peak of beauty, provided a welcome burst of color against the gloom. Their fragrance perfumed the air. Karen was radiant in a pale blue silk suit. A matching wide-brimmed gauzy hat framed her face. Of course she wore the diamond star.

When Nigel saw her, he said, "I'm not at all surprised the day is overcast. It's obvious all the blue has left heaven and gone into your eyes."

Karen hardly heard the words of the simple civil ceremony. She was almost surprised when she saw Nigel leaning towards her to take his kiss. "We're actually married." Karen whispered, still not quite believing her luck.

"Yes we are, Mrs. Craxford."

They chose the slower route, and so arrived late in the evening. They pulled up to a remote cottage on a bluff high above the sea. It was too dark to see anything, but they could hear the waves breaking against the coastline far below. The headlights shone on a weathered sign hanging from a lamppost. MOUSE SEA, it read.

"Mouse Sea." Her laughter was uncontrollable. "You have got to be kidding me. It's not bad enough to live in Mousehole, but you have to name your cottage that?"

"It wasn't me," protested Nigel, joining in her laughter, "I told you it's been in my family for years. The story is that a little child, who lived here long ago, had a beloved pet mouse who died. The name is supposed to be in memory of that mouse. No one has ever had the heart to change it."

"You've got a kinder heart than I have."

Nigel unpacked all the luggage from the car and piled it on the front step. He put in the key, and pushed open the reluctant front door. He then went from room to room, turning on the lights so Karen could see. The comfortably furnished rooms, cozy in the lamp light, welcomed her. She looked at Nigel in gratitude. She was home.

The morning brought new delight to Karen. A small garden hugged the house, the sea sparkled through the windows. Broken bits of sunlight floated on the water's surface.

"This view is incredible, you can look out over the water and see forever." He joined her at the window and followed her gaze.

"So true," he thought.

Karen's honeymoon was blissful. Days were spent exploring the village and surrounding countryside. Nights, after simple suppers they made together, were spent making love, locked in each other's arms.

Every morning Nigel presented her with some small thoughtful present. After they had been there almost a week, Nigel announced "I have one last surprise for you." He took her down a twisted path that led to a cove. Tied up on the rock-strewn sand, was a small launch.

"Get in." he ordered.

She was momentarily taken aback at the tone of his voice. Obediently, she climbed in. Now Nigel was grinning widely. They motored around a bend and followed the coast until they entered Mousehole Harbour. He brought the launch alongside an obviously new boat, a fifty-foot sleek beauty. A flight of crying gulls circled overhead. The sea wind, whipped her dark hair across her face. Nigel pointed to the name written on the side of the boat. STAR OF THE SEA. "It's yours!" he said proudly. "I bought it for you."

"You did this just for me?" Karen was overcome with tears.

"Absolutely."

That night, after dinner, Nigel did not want to make love. Instead, he took a book from a crowded bookshelf, seated himself in an easy chair next to the empty hearth, and read out loud to her.

Do not go gentle into that good night

Rage, rage against the dying of the light.

Karen was disturbed by his selection. "Why would you choose such a gloomy poem to read to me, especially on our honeymoon?"

"I like to read Dylan Thomas whenever I'm here. It's really a fitting tribute to our honeymoon, since as I told you before, he also spent his honeymoon here."

That's also when he told her he wanted to spend the next day and night on their new boat. "We need to take advantage of the last of the good weather. It can get quite windy and chilly out at sea."

In the morning, packing up her clothing and provisions needed for the boat, Karen felt reluctant to leave. "I feel like I'm in a storybook here. Cinderella and Prince Charming come to mind, but instead of a castle there's a cottage. Actually, I prefer the cottage. I just hope it all doesn't come to an end at midnight."

"Not to worry," Nigel kissed her forehead, "I can promise you I'll still be here in the morning."

They left the harbour and soon lost sight of land. Nigel kept going. He handled the boat with expertise as he stayed on course. The weather was cool and clear, the sea calm. Late in the day they dropped anchor and prepared their evening meal. They ate on deck and watched the light leave the world. As it grew dark, they leaned together against the rail and gazed up at the stars, brilliant in the night sky. There still was no sight of land and they hadn't seen another boat for hours.

"Does anyone out there know where we are?"

"I hope not."

Later Karen was relieved when he wanted to make love again. Afterwards, lying in his arms, she only half jokingly said "Last night I was afraid you had gotten tired of me."

"I will never get tired of you, my darling girl. I can swear to that." The boat rocked gently in the waves. The movement of the sea lulled Karen into deep, dreamless slumber. The night, lit by ghosts of long dead stars, grew cold. Karen shivered in her sleep and awoke with a chill. She saw Nigel standing over her. She never saw the morning sun.

PART TWO

UNRAVELED

The slamming of the door in the upstairs flat, accompanied by the usual angry shouts, startled Elizabeth out of sleep and into another day. "Why bother setting my alarm?" she wondered. "The fucking neighbors start fighting every morning at 5:30 am. Why the hell do they stay together? I hope they don't think it's for the children's sake. My parents used that excuse for years. I'm living proof it's not a winning strategy."

Elizabeth, sleep deprived, as usual, dragged herself into the shower. That usually helped her revive somewhat. Looking at her reflection in the bathroom mirror was also not a good way to start her day. In spite of all the tips she tried to get from fashion magazines on how to look her best, she never got the results she wanted. The advice was often to play up what nature gave you, not to try to look like someone else. *Be the best you can be.* That was in the last article she had read. But what she had to work with, or against, was a short, stocky build, an ordinary face and a prominent nose.

Her hair was straight and silky, but the color of a field mouse. No matter what makeup she used, she never liked the results. "I really need to have my hair and makeup done by a professional," she thought. But a policewoman's salary didn't allow for such luxuries, especially when she was saving every extra pound she had to buy a quiet new flat in a better neighborhood. She thought she'd be able to start looking after her next paycheck. But even then, she'd have to keep up the payments on a more expensive place. She saw no way to fulfill her wish to pamper herself, no matter how much she felt she deserved it. A divorced woman in her early forties, with no children and no prospects, her future did not look bright.

In spite of that, she was not yet ready to give up on life. She had read too many stories where people who had nothing, wound up having their dreams come true. On the commute to work, as she was jostled along her route by the swaying of the train and other commuters pushing past her, she read an article about an entrepreneur who had started with nothing. When asked the difference between people who became rich and those who remained poor, his answer was, "Poor people spend their money, rich people invest their money." She hoped the money she had saved for the new flat fell into the investment category.

As she stepped out of the train and on to the platform, she was blasted by gusts of damp chilly air. Some rubbish that had been dropped on the sidewalk blew across her path. Instinctively, she reached down, picked it up and dropped it into a nearby receptacle. "Maybe that's what attracted me to police work," she thought, "I like getting rubbish off the street." Early spring weather was unpredictable, and coming out of the windy streets into police headquarters brought little relief. The atmosphere inside the gray non-descript building was also chilly. Her fellow police officers did not warm to an ambitious, smart woman who was determined to become a detective. She had been passed over several times, in spite of earning high scores on her tests. The excuse had always been seniority, but since she started working there almost fifteen years ago, that excuse was becoming harder to justify.

"Good morning Officer Higgins," some of the men smirked while greeting her. When they talked among themselves, it was always first names or nick-names. They never called her by her first name, or her nick-name.

They called her 'Professor Higgins' behind her back. She was constantly looking for ways to improve herself, so they named her after the character in 'My Fair Lady,' who transformed Eliza Doolittle.

The hostile work environment, her abusive alcoholic father, and her cheating ex-husband, had turned her into a man-hater. The fact that she worked in a department that investigated scams and fraud, most of which were perpetrated by men, only hardened her attitude. Sometimes, when a woman scammed a man, she secretly cheered her on. "Way to go! The bastard probably had it coming." Of course, she pretended neutrality as she investigated the case, but wasn't at all sorry when a woman "got away with murder."

She heard laughter coming from the men at the front desk, then someone said, "This is just the case for Officer Higgins." Soon after, Sgt. Michael Boyle escorted a man in to see her. He appeared uneasy, fidgeting with the cap he held in his hands. In spite of her opinion about men, this one didn't arouse her hostility. He had a mild, kindly face. She introduced herself and invited him to sit in one of the two uncomfortable metal folding chairs facing her desk. "How can I help you?"

"I'm not sure I should have even come, and from the reaction of the people at the front desk, I feel more than a little foolish being here." "Pay no attention to them. That's just their way. Besides, you're already here. Something must have seemed important enough to bring you to the police."

"Well, actually, it was my wife who thought I should come. After thirty-eight years of marriage, I've come to appreciate her good judgement. She often sees things I'm not even aware of."

A man who pays attention to his wife. Elizabeth was beginning to like him.

"I'm Hugh Beasley," he continued. "I have an antique shop on Winkley Street. We restore antiques and do weaving, mostly to repair old fabrics. I've had this customer who's been to my shop about four times now over the last three years. He first came to have me weave a tapestry that looks like it was an antique from the Middle Ages. He deliberately wanted it to look worn. I've done work like that before. Sometimes people like to pretend to have an ancient pedigree and hang fakes in their home to show off. His request was unusual because he wanted to have the tapestry be a portrait of a man and woman, and gave me photographs of what they should look like. One of the pictures was of him, the other I assumed was his wife. I thought that he was an eccentric who wanted to give his wife a unique gift. But it was so unusual that I wouldn't even begin such a project, and risk that the customer wouldn't come back to pay for it, unless I was paid in full. He didn't care at all about the expense, and paid in advance without any objection. I asked him his name, but he didn't want to give it to me. Since he'd already paid, he didn't see the need. I explained that I wanted it for a record of his order, so that when he came back for it, whoever was here could find it for him. He then said his name was Neal Crawford, but I never asked for any identity. As long as I had my money, what did I care? He didn't even want a receipt, just said he'd be back on the date I told him the order would be ready. When he came for the tapestry, he also wanted the photographs he'd left with me. I gave them back, but didn't tell him that I'd made copies of them for my files. I like to have back-ups of everything." He shifted his considerable weight in the undersized metal chair. "Well," he went on, "I didn't give him any more thought, but he came back again about eight months later with a somewhat different request. He had the tapestry with him, as well as a photograph of a different woman. This time he wanted only the woman's face replaced. I was thinking, perhaps he had divorced or broken up with the woman in the tapestry. Again, he paid up front, and again asked for the photograph back when the tapestry was ready. I first told my wife about him when he came back for the third time with the same request. She thought it was strange, and only half kidding, asked if I thought he could be a serial killer, you know like Bluebeard, the rich man who killed seven of his wives."

"Yes, I know the Bluebeard story. Let's hope he isn't like that."

Hugh Beasley said he laughed when she said that.

"When did you think she might be right?"

"When he came back for the fourth time, just a few days ago, even I began to wonder what he was up to. That's when my wife urged me to report this."

Elizabeth leaned forward, "It's certainly odd behavior. It could just be his way of getting women to like him."

"I wouldn't think he'd need much help in that department. He's very good looking, even I noticed that."

"I'll do a quick search on Neal Crawford and let you know if I find anything. I really appreciate your coming to the police. You never know when something actually is a problem. Thank your wife for being so vigilant. I'll need a description from you and your contact information."

After Hugh Beasley left, Elizabeth found eleven Neal Crawfords who could possibly fit the profile. She spent the next several days checking them out. All proved to be dead-ends. The men in her department had been making fun of the whole story. "Probably just a rich eccentric who likes to play dress up with his girl friends," was their verdict.

Anything was possible; however, she was hoping Mrs. Beasley was right. She relished the possibility that she could make her fellow officers look like fools.

Entering the antique shop, she saw Hugh behind the counter. "I didn't find any Neal Crawfords, but it's quite likely he was using an alias, since he went to such trouble to keep a low profile. If you'll give me a picture of him, and the latest photograph he gave you, I'll check it for fingerprints. I'd also like copies of the pictures of the other women. Are there any other details that you might have overlooked?"

Starting to shake his head no, he stopped. "Wait, the time before this, he had the photograph in his wallet, the other times he had just handed them to me. When he took it out, a credit card slip from The King's Grill fell out onto the counter. Just to make conversation, I mentioned that I've taken my wife there on special occasions. It's a nice treat for her, you know," he seemed pleased to tell Elizabeth that.

Could it be possible that there were actually some nice men in the world? "Do you know the date?" was all she said.

"I'll get it from my file. So you think there might be something to my wife's suspicions? She'll be so pleased to hear how seriously you're taking this."

"I'll be in touch if I need any more information from you. Good-bye, Mr. Beasley."

"Please call me Hugh."

She smiled and walked out into the street. When Elizabeth got back to her office, she ran a fingerprint check. She found a match! His name was Nigel Craxford, and his crime was a one-off scam of a female pensioner. He had received a light sentence sixteen years ago, and had no further record.

The picture on file was a younger version of the one she had of him. Although his prior conviction involved no violence, and had been a long time ago, she had a hunch that this was worth following up.

She walked quickly through the crowded city streets, pushing against the blustery wind. Empty branches swayed wildly overhead. The trees waited for warmth before sending their delicate buds into the world. She didn't have that luxury. Fortunately, she didn't have too far to go.

She looked forward to continuing her investigation at The King's Grill, located in the Hotel Raphael. It was not the kind of place her work or her budget had enabled her to go to before. Elizabeth gave herself a few moments to enjoy the atmosphere of the famous restaurant before approaching the headwaiter. She admired the crystal chandeliers that hung from the tall ceiling. They sparkled brightly against the mellow wood paneling on the walls. Tall narrow windows, overlooking a landscaped courtyard, were framed by raw silk, cream colored draperies. The tables were set with fine china, gleaming silver and crystal glassware. Large flower arrangements were scattered around the room, adding fragrance as well as beauty.

"So this is how the other one percent lives. I sure would like to figure out how they got here, and how I can join them." Even a promotion to detective wouldn't allow for this lifestyle. The contrast between this world and hers fueled her frustration.

The headwaiter was cooperative. He recognized Nigel Craxford from the picture she showed him. He said he made it a point to remember regular customers, but Nigel was especially easy to remember because of his film-star looks. "I also wondered why a man as handsome as he is was usually with very plain or even unattractive women. Only one time did I see him with a pretty one." He looked at the pictures Elizabeth showed him and, pointing to one, said, "I think that's the pretty one, but I'm not entirely certain. She might have been staying at the hotel. Is he in some kind of trouble?"

"I can't discuss it, but I would appreciate your not saying anything to him if he comes in again. I'd also like you to call me right away if he does. Here's the number to call," handing him her card. "And please, keep this conversation to yourself."

Elizabeth left through the double doors that led into the hotel lobby. She walked across the highly polished marble floor to the ornately carved reception desk. No one else in the lobby seemed to be aware of the opulence around them. "Imagine taking all this for granted!" It seemed inconceivable. One of the people who worked at the reception desk recognized Nigel and the same woman the headwaiter thought he remembered. The rest of the employees she questioned didn't recognize anyone.

The pretty woman's name was Karen Miller, a rich American who had extended her stay in one of their suites by several weeks. The concierge said he had become friendly with her during that time. "She was just lovely. She obviously had a lot of money, but treated everyone kindly and with respect. You don't always see that kind of behavior among the very rich. Sometimes the guests act like we're their slaves, making all sorts of unreasonable demands at all hours. That was never Mrs. Miller."

"Mrs. Miller? Somehow I thought she was single, since she was with this man."

"She was widowed, she told me."

"Oh."

"Has anything happened to her? Is that why you're asking all these questions?"

"I really can't say anything now. I'd like to talk to the other people here who might have remembered her."

"You should see Angela Barrett, she's right over there."

"It's funny you should be asking about her," Angela said. "I was just thinking about her the other day."

"Why was that?"

"She was so excited one day and said she just had to share her good news or would burst. We had become friendly by then. She was planning to get married to that man you showed me in the picture. She had promised him to keep it a secret, even from her daughter in America, until after the wedding. The reason she told me about their marriage plans is that she wanted to book a week in the same suite she was in now, as a surprise for her future husband's birthday. He loved London, and she thought it would be romantic to spend the time after they were married in a place that was so important to them during their courtship. His birthday wasn't until three months after their wedding, but she wanted to make sure she could get the suite she wanted. She made the reservation in the name of Mr. and Mrs. Nigel Craxford, even paid for it in advance. But when that date arrived, they never checked in. I called the cell phone number she had given me, and got a message it was not a working number. It seemed so out of character for her not to let us know if her plans had changed. Anyway, the reservation was for exactly a year ago last week, so I thought about it then. I remembered the date because it's the same date as my daughter's birthday. I also remember now that I asked her how she could keep a secret like that from her daughter. I know how close I am with mine, now that she's past those teenage years. Karen had laughed, and said it was difficult, but thought how exciting it was going to be to come back home and surprise her daughter with her new husband. Her plan was to call her daughter when she checked out of here, and then call her after the wedding to let her know when she'd be coming back home. I hope she's ok."

"Thanks for all your cooperation. I'll be in touch if I need anything else. Here's my card, call if you hear from Karen Miller or Nigel Craxford." She also asked Angela Barrett not to discuss this with anyone else.

All the women in the photographs, except Karen, were not very good looking. This would most likely make them more vulnerable to a man like Nigel, especially if he were charming, which she suspected he was. He probably had a talent for spotting weakness. If I could talk to her daughter in America, it might give me some insight into Karen. It shouldn't be too difficult to find the daughter, since she had gotten Karen's home address from the hotel. She was confident the Allentown, Pennsylvania police department would be able to give her that information. It would also be useful to see if they could add anything to her inquiry.

Coming home to her cramped flat after being at The King's Grill and the Raphael was more difficult than usual. The contrast between 'the good life' and her life was overwhelming. Her mind raced, "Maybe I'm about to crack open a sensational case that will make me famous. I could have a movie producer interested in making it into a film. Then I'd get rich, quit my job, leave the country, get plastic surgery and have a complete makeover." Sometimes it was her craziest thoughts that kept her sane.

Of course, Nigel Craxford could turn out to be a completely harmless person, a lonely man looking for love. If that's the case, I'm just his type. "Yeah, right," she thought.

She went into her tiny kitchen and reheated some takeout food left over from the night before. Too exhausted to make herself a proper meal, she collapsed onto her sofa and turned on the television. The evening news was just starting. The usual terrible events of the day played out on the screen. "I don't think I need to see this," she thought, and was about to change the channel when a picture of a woman came on. The newswoman identified her as forty-eight-year-old Evelyn Wiley. She had died of apparent smoke inhalation, after a fire started by an elderly man in the flat below her had fallen asleep while smoking. The fire department was still investigating. Elizabeth bolted upright on her sofa. Evelyn Wiley was the same woman in the latest photograph that Nigel Craxford had given Hugh Beasley. Could Nigel have had anything to do with the fire, and made it look like an accident? But that seemed odd, the tapestry wasn't finished yet. Her theory was that he needed to use the tapestry in some way to ensnare his victims. A neighbor of the dead woman was being interviewed, "She was very quiet, kept to herself. As far as I know she never married, and had no family. Poor soul didn't seem to have much of a life. But what's really tragic is that she recently won a large amount of money from the national lottery. She didn't like the publicity she got right after it. I told her no one ever remembers the winners, except relatives looking for a handout. Anyway, she told me only a few days ago that her luck seems to have changed completely and she expected she'd be moving before too long. She didn't give any details, but it's the first time I'd seen her look so happy. And now this, poor soul." The neighbor shook her head sadly. A commercial for a cruise line came on. Stunned, Elizabeth turned off the television.

The next morning, she arrived at her office earlier than usual, eager to be at work even though she couldn't call America until the afternoon. The phone was already ringing as she reached her desk.

"Officer Higgins," she said answering her phone.

It was Hugh Beasley. He sounded excited. "I just got into work, and before I could even take off my coat, Neal Crawford called. He cancelled the work on the tapestry, and said he'd stop by to pick it up as soon as he got back to London. His phone number was displayed on my phone. I thought you'd want it."

"I certainly do. Did you see last night's news?"

"No, my wife and I went to an early movie."

"The woman, whose photograph you have now, died yesterday of smoke inhalation. That probably explains why he cancelled his order. I'll be in to see you a little later today. Will you be available?"

"I'll be here all day."

Elizabeth made her call to the Allentown police department. It was easier than she thought to get the information she wanted. Karen Miller had been well known in the town. Her late husband had owned the region's largest trucking company, and her daughter Lori, a lawyer, was married to Nick Brenner, a successful real estate developer. Karen's tragic death while on vacation in the UK had been reported in all the local papers. The policeman she was talking to knew a neighbor of Lori's. That neighbor had told him she was still mourning her mother's death, and hadn't been able to return to her law practice yet. The policeman suggested that Elizabeth should go easy with Lori. Elizabeth, not surprised that Karen was dead, thanked him and called Lori Brenner.

"Hello." A young woman's voice answered the phone. "May I speak to Lori Brenner."

"Speaking, who is this?" A baby cried in the background.

"This is Officer Elizabeth Higgins with the London police. I'd like to talk to you about your mother, Karen Miller. I'm sorry for your loss."

Lori started to cry. "I'm sorry, I'm still very upset over her death."

"No need to apologize. I'm calling because I'm investigating a man your mother was planning to marry while she was in the UK. From what I've been able to learn, she was keeping it a secret from you so she could surprise you when she went back home. Were you aware of any of this?"

Lori had so many doubts about what actually happened to her mother, doubts that no one else shared. Knowing that someone else was looking into the circumstances of her death came as a tremendous relief.

"All I know was that she said she'd met someone, was having fun, but it was nothing serious. I suspected there was more to the story than she was letting on. I was going to go over there to find out what was really happening, but then I learned that I was pregnant and had some complications that prevented me from travelling for a while, so I didn't have a chance to help her. But you know what else really haunts me? I was the one who insisted that she take this trip. I even gave her a diamond star pendant, told her it would bring her luck. She didn't want to go. I pushed her into it. If I hadn't done that I'd still have a mother." Lori broke down at this point. "She never even got to meet her grandson!" she sobbed. She regained her composure enough to continue. "My mother called me regularly, told me she was checking out of her hotel and would call back in a few days to let me know when she'd be corning home. I was so excited. But then I never heard from her again. A few days after she was supposed to call me and didn't, I was frantic. I called the hotel, I called the police. I was about to hire a private investigator, when I got a call from a lawyer, Simon Blair. He said he had sad news about my mother. She had died in a boating accident while on her honeymoon. He knew where to reach me because he had drawn up a new will for her while she was in London. Lori spoke nervously, her voice quavering. "Do you think he killed my mother, is that why you're calling?"

"Why don't you finish your story," Elizabeth gently suggested.

"Simon Blair told me that she and this man, Nigel Craxford, had come to him to make out their wills. Simon Blair reassured me that there was nothing sinister about Nigel. "In fact," he had said, "he wanted to leave everything to your mother, and in my office, he was telling your mother he didn't want her to change her will. He even asked me to talk her out of it. She was the one who insisted on going through with it. Nigel wanted her to have everything he owned, in case anything happened to him. Even though he knew you had more money than you could ever spend, he said you should be the only one to inherit whatever she had." The solicitor claimed Nigel was inconsolable after the accident, hardly able to function." He sent Lori a copy of the will, which was legitimate. His law firm turned out to be an old established one with an excellent reputation. Everything seemed to confirm that it was just a tragic accident, yet Lori could never quite believe it.

"What was your mother like?"

"She was wonderful, loving, kind, generous. The best mother anyone could ever have. She would have made a fabulous grandmother." Lori started to cry again.

"Was your mother a confident woman, or shy? What was her personality like?"

"She never really appreciated her own worth. She lived in my father's shadow and had largely retreated from the world. I was afraid she might be naïve about men, since my father was her only boyfriend, and they married so young."

Elizabeth got the description she was expecting. A rich insecure widow was an easy target. Nigel might have been inconsolable after her death, but still he managed to pull himself together enough to collect his inheritance. In this case, money was a powerful motive, and being alone on the boat was the ideal opportunity. Now she needed evidence. She couldn't, and wouldn't, do anything without it.

Elizabeth made an appointment to question Simon Blair.

He graciously made time for her, and patiently repeated the same details he had gone over with Lori.

"In fact," he said, "Nigel called me a few days later about another matter I was handling for him, and during that conversation I learned why it was so important for him to leave Karen everything he had. He said that many years ago, he had been married and had a young daughter. They were all on a trip to Italy, in

Sienna, and while he was driving, a drunk driver lost control of his car and crashed into them. Both his wife and daughter were killed. He was grief stricken, not only were they dead, but he felt responsible because he was at the wheel. Even though it had been almost eighteen years, he said he still felt guilty. It made him feel better to take care of Karen any way he could. If you could have spoken with him after the boating accident, you would have realized the pain he was in. He was barely able to speak or function. He said it happened while they were on their honeymoon. What made the accident even more devastating for him was that he'd bought the boat as a surprise for Karen. He said she wasn't familiar with the boat, got up during the night and tripped on some rope that was lying on deck. He thinks she probably tripped when the boat pitched in the rough seas. He asked me to let Karen's daughter know what had happened since he couldn't bear to make such a horrible call. This isn't the behavior of a cold-blooded killer. The man was beyond distraught, I assure you."

Elizabeth thanked Simon Blair for his seeing her, especially at such short notice.

"I hope I was able to clear things up for you."

"The information you gave me was very helpful. Thank you again."

Evelyn Wiley's death bought a little time before Craxford would find another victim. Further investigation into the fire proved it was accidental. But the fact that Evelyn Wiley had come into money shortly before she died convinced Elizabeth that Nigel's interest in her was purely monetary. Her instinct told that her that he was a killer. She was certain he'd soon be on the prowl for another victim. He worked fast, so she would have to work faster.

"I'll put a stop to you, you bastard." she thought, determined to get this ruthless man before he killed again.

Elizabeth enjoyed working with Judge Connelly. Sarah Connelly had come up the hard way. Graduating first in her law school class, she was too talented and too forceful to be held back by anyone. Elizabeth looked around the office as she waited for the judge to finish a phone call. Sunbeams streaming through the windows picked out dust motes dancing in the air, and shone on a silver gavel that rested on her desk. It had been a gift from her husband when she was first appointed to the bench. She kept it highly polished, never wanting to tarnish the law. Her massive wooden desk was generally strewn with empty coffee cups, open law books and files for the proceedings scheduled for the coming weeks. She worked as hard now as when she had first come on the bench, taking her responsibilities to uphold the law and seek justice with unwavering determination. Even those who didn't like the results of her rulings, knew they had gotten a fair hearing.

Besides telling Judge Connelly about Nigel's odd behavior involving the tapestry, his alias and past criminal record, Elizabeth reported her conversation with Lori Brenner.

"After talking to Lori Brenner, I thought it was important to speak with Simon Blair. He told me that Nigel Craxford called him before the accident about another matter he was handling. Craxford then let him know why he wanted to make Karen Miller his beneficiary. He claimed to have been married before, and that his wife and child were killed by a drunk driver in Italy. I couldn't find any records of that accident. He also claimed that rough seas probably contributed to Karen Miller's death. I checked the weather reports for conditions that night.

There was a light wind and the sea was calm. I've got proof he's a liar. Now I've got to prove he's a killer."

Elizabeth left Judge Connelly's chambers with the court's permission to monitor Craxford's credit card and tap his phone.

"It shouldn't be hard to keep tabs on him. He'll be out of circulation soon. I just hope it's soon enough."

Nigel finished unpacking and dressing for dinner. Starting the hunt for new conquests always gave him a rush. He didn't need money anymore, but did need the thrill of seducing his victims. Inheriting their money after he killed them was his way of keeping score. Even at boarding school, no one ever caught on to his schemes. The only exception was when he was arrested for scamming a pensioner. He had been sloppy then, but had since perfected his technique. He had no remorse for taking lives. "Pathetic cows," he called his victims, except Karen. He thought she had just been a naïve fool. He thought no one was his equal, and that he was superior to anyone he had ever met. Born in the winter of his father's life, he was like a winter sun, all brilliance and no warmth. He looked casually elegant in his perfectly tailored clothing. Wearing a pale blue shirt, dark blue blazer and gray wool trousers, he admired his reflection in the stateroom mirror. The shirt complimented his ice blue eyes. He had yet to meet the woman who was immune to his deadly combination of looks and charm. This cruise was the perfect vehicle for him, an exclusive holiday for adults only. In all probability, lonely rich women would outnumber the men on board. This was almost going to be too easy. After investing his time with that dreadfully dull Evelyn Wiley and having it 'all go up in smoke' (he found that phrase amusing) he felt entitled to an easy conquest. One last look in the mirror, then 'show time.'

Nigel had arranged to be seated at the captain's table. It's where he expected to find the wealthiest passengers. There were ten of them including the captain. Two balding, graying men wearing glasses, and six women, ranging in looks from plain to ugly. He and one other woman were the only ones under sixty. One of the older ones who was seated to his left appeared to be wearing the entire contents of a small jewelry store. She was thrilled when he danced with her after dinner.

Late in the afternoon of the following day, Nigel found a sunny spot on deck and luxuriously stretched out on a lounge chair, enjoying the warmth of the late day sun. Tonight he'd begin to seriously pursue his quarry. Before he could close his eyes, the only woman at his table under sixty sat down in the chair next to his. The liquor on her breath was overpowering. Sipping from a flask she held in her hand, she appeared tipsy and talkative, not a good combination.

"Oh, hi," she said, oblivious that she was intruding. "You were at my table last night, weren't you?"

He nodded, remaining silent. He hoped to discourage further conversation. She was not discouraged.

"Aren't you loving this ship?" She didn't wait for an answer, but kept up her prattle. "I think it's so interesting meeting new people. I love all the dirt you learn. Knowing you're not going to see anyone after you get back home, you can say all kinds of things." She slurred her words. "I think maybe I had a little too much of this." She laughed and waved her flask in the air. A waiter approached her and asked if she'd like something from the bar, in a glass. "No, this way I know what's in my drink." She brought her face close to his, assaulting him with her breath. She lowered her voice, "I'll let you in on a secret," a confidence he hadn't asked for, "in the spa today, talking to some of the ladies, I found out that the woman in the stateroom next to mine is on board with a man who's not her husband." More laughter directed more foul breath in his face. Nigel winced.

"I think I'll have to kill her here and now, in front of everyone. I might even get knighted by the Queen for service to the nation."

"You know what else I found out? The woman you were dancing with last night, the one with all the jewelry, none of it is hers. She's not even rich." The drunk woman howled with laughter. "Her husband died almost a year ago, she took the life insurance money and spent it all on this cruise. She's pretending to be rich. All that jewelry belongs to her friends. She doesn't have a pot to piss in." She cackled, apparently this was the funniest thing she had ever heard. Just as suddenly as she had started laughing, she grew maudlin. Tears came to her eyes, "At least she had a husband and friends. So what if she doesn't have money. It doesn't always bring happiness. My parents left me a lot of money, and I'm still unhappy. I never married or had children." She was planning to continue her self-pitying monologue, when suddenly she got up and doubled over. "Oh, I think I'm going to be sick!" She staggered away, clutching her stomach.

She didn't show up at the captain's table that night. The passengers dined mostly in silence. The drunk woman's seat was empty, Nigel was quiet and distracted, and the bejeweled woman was clearly disappointed that he wasn't showing any interest in her. No one else knew how or cared much about keeping conversation alive.

Nigel pulled his cap lower, shielding his eyes from the sun glare bouncing off the water. He walked easily on the rolling deck, enjoying the salty wind blowing against his face. Approaching from the opposite direction was the woman who'd been drunk yesterday afternoon. She appeared sober now. Her short strides were steady in spite of the heavy swells. She turned her head away in embarrassment, trying to avoid him. It was too late.

"Good morning. You didn't come to dinner last night, are you ok?"

"Except for my hangover, I'm fine. I have to apologize for yesterday. I'm so ashamed of myself. I can't remember exactly what I said, but I don't think I had any more to drink than usual. The reason I carry a flask is so I can control what's in my drink. You hear all these scary stories now about men drugging drinks. It's the first time this has ever happened. I was on painkillers after dental work, and I thought I'd waited long enough after my last dose to start drinking. Apparently, I was wrong. I guess the combination was a disaster. Again, I apologize for anything I might have said. Maybe it's better I don't remember." She had a need to redeem herself in his eyes.

"We all have things we'd like to forget, don't give it another thought."

"But you know," she was clearly still concerned, "I'm really bothered by yesterday. Did I make a complete fool of myself, air any dirty laundry?"

Nigel smiled reassuringly, "The only thing you said was that there was someone you met who's here with a man who wasn't her husband. You didn't name names, you didn't give away any state secrets."

"That's a relief. Sometimes alcohol is like truth serum."

"And what's the truth you're hiding?" he teased.

"Oh, I can't go there," she laughed.

"I didn't catch your name at dinner the other night. The lady sitting next to me was talking. I'm Nigel Craxford, and now that I'm really looking at you, I think we might have met before. "

"I don't think so. I would definitely have remembered meeting you."

"I hope that's meant as a compliment."

"It is."

"I still didn't get your name."

"Bess..."

The ship lurched violently in the growing turbulence, toppling an elderly man who had been standing nearby. His wife, a dumpy dyed blonde, screamed as she anxiously waddled around her injured husband. She wore a disapproving expression, always on the lookout for a reason to be dissatisfied. She was satisfied to have found one.

"They should never have made the deck so slippery. No wonder my husband fell. Wait until I call my solicitor."

Last night Nigel had overheard her complaining to her waiter that everything on the menu disagreed with her. In spite of her obvious face-lift, no surgeon was skillful enough to lift the comers of her mouth. Before Bess could finish answering, Nigel left to help the fallen man. Looking back over his shoulder, he called out, "I'll catch up with you later." As he reached the couple, the disgruntled wife was still going on about the unsafe conditions onboard the ship.

"Why don't we get your husband to the infirmary, and worry about calling your solicitor later?"

They didn't see each other until dinner.

"So, knight in shining armor, how is the old man?"

"He'll be fine. He just needed a couple of stitches on his forehead. I think his wife was let down that she wouldn't be able to sue the cruise line for a lot of money. She was probably hoping to make a killing."

"A little concern for her husband would have been nice. What a world!" Bess shook her head. "Nothing surprises me anymore."

"I hope I can surprise you." Nigel, his eyes twinkling, lifted his wine glass, and clinked it against hers."

"Here's to surprises." Bess drained her glass.

When Bess had booked passage on this cruise, she was on a manhunt. She had invested time and money, coming home empty-handed was not an option. She now had reason for optimism.

Nigel was attentive and charming all during dinner. He was very interested in getting to know Bess. She was happy to tell her story. He learned the family money had come from the sale of her parent's chain of successful grocery stores. She didn't tell him directly how wealthy she was. But reading between the lines of her story, he found out all he needed to know.

They danced late into the night, laughing and talking. He pressed her close and whispered how wonderful it was being with her.

"It's like we've known each other before. I'm so happy to be with you."

When the music ended, Bess looked at Nigel curiously.

"What is it about me you like so much? I can't believe you've ever met a woman who didn't fall for you. I'm not so attractive. I hope you don't mind my being blunt, but I'm too old for games, and never liked them even when I was younger. You could do a lot better than me."

"That's exactly why I like you. You're refreshing, honest. There's no pretense with you. What you see is what you get, and I hope I can get you. Beauty can wear thin. A lot of beautiful women are too self involved. They think the world revolves around them. You've lived, you know how to get around without relying on a man. I'm impressed. You're smart and independent. In fact, your name suits you, like Good Queen Bess. She was able to out-maneuver all the men who wanted to marry her just to get to the throne. That's the kind of woman I admire, and want. Does that answer your question?"

"Yes." Bess seemed convinced. "And I have to admit, now it's my turn to be impressed. The men I've met before practically ran me over in their rush to get to all the pretty girls wearing tight jeans. I'm glad I met you. You're not like the others."

They were inseparable from then on. Spontaneous and playful, they seemed to share the same interests. They would talk into the early hours of the morning. Nigel was surprised that Bess was so attuned to him. She was very observant, nothing escaped her. In spite of their compatibility, she wouldn't allow him to make love to her. "It's too soon. I want to see where we are after this holiday is over." Nigel was relieved, having to make love to his victims, with the exception of Karen, wasn't enjoyable. It was a necessary evil. Bess wondered aloud if he'd want to see her after the cruise ended. She didn't have to worry, Nigel assured her, they were a couple.

"I'm not going to get rid of you."

"I know that now, but I'd still like to wait a little while longer to make love to you." She wouldn't be all that bad if she had a plastic surgeon work on her nose. He thought it was curious that someone with all her money hadn't had it fixed. Maybe she was afraid to go under the knife. Whatever her reason, he was happy to accommodate her.

"Here's a perfect spot for a picture. Lean against the railing and look straight ahead. I'm a pretty good photographer, I think you'll like the results." Nigel had an expensive camera that he enjoyed using, and was eager to take her picture.

"No way! I hate being photographed. I never look good."

Bess's reaction was surprising. Most women were flattered by this request. She kept moving, making it impossible for him to get a picture. He would need it soon for the tapestry, but he still had some time.

The last night of the voyage, Bess surprised him again. They were about to say good night, when she reached out and lightly touched his arm.

"Don't go yet." She took a deep breath and hesitated for a moment. "You said you liked that I was honest, so I'm just going to come out and tell you what I'm thinking. I'm thinking we should get married. Before you object, let me go on. We're not kids, we've lived long enough to know that it's hard to find love. I hate to waste time playing games. I know what I want, and what I want is you." She looked anxiously at him for his answer.

"You do go for what you want." This woman was surprisingly bold.

"Well, so do I, and luckily, we both want the same thing. Consider yourself engaged!"

Nigel was delighted. He wouldn't even have to bother with the tapestry this time. It wasn't his usual routine, but he was happy to speed up the process. She told him she wanted to be married as soon as possible. Bess had thought about all the arrangements. She was good at planning ahead.

"Since it's where we met, I'd like to get married on this ship, when it next sails. The captain can perform the ceremony, and we don't have to go anywhere else for the honeymoon. It sails again one week after we land. I'm pretty sure we could book a stateroom, they're so expensive, something should be available."

He agreed with her. Nigel then became serious. "Before we get married you need to know something about me. So far, it's been all fun and games with us. But if we're going to have a future, you have to know about my past. I married my childhood sweetheart, Joyce. We had twin boys, our life was wonderful. In those years I did a lot of travelling for my import-export business. I had a trip planned to America, actually, California. The boys, Kenny and Paul, were eight years old and obsessed with cowboys. So I decided to bring the family along and drive to Arizona after my business was done. We went to a rodeo, a ghost town and visited all the sights we knew the boys would love. On the last day, our trip was over, we were on our way to the airport, when out of nowhere a drunk driver crashed into our car. Joyce and the boys were killed instantly. I was knocked unconscious and fractured my ribs. I recovered from my injuries, but never got over the guilt. My whole family died while I was driving. I couldn't protect them." Nigel was silent and held his head in his hands.

Finally he looked up and continued. "I let my family down. I need to know I can take care of you. I have a lot of money and no one to spend it on."

"You never let your family down! What a horrible story! Unbelievable!"

"Listen, I need to know if anything happens to me, you'll be well taken care of. I want to make a new will leaving you everything I have."

Bess interrupted. "That won't bring your family back. Besides, I'm rich. My parents left me in great shape. I don't need anything from you."

"Bess, I need this from you. Please, it'll help me to know that I'm protecting you anyway I can. If you don't need the money, you could give it to charity. Bess, please do this for me," he begged.

"All right, but on one condition, I have to do the same for you. We should start our married life as equals. What you do, I should be able to do. And one more thing, no prenup either. This is 'til death do we part."

"I want that too."

He fell into her arms, and reluctantly agreed to her demands. "I'll email my solicitor and try to arrange a meeting with him after we dock tomorrow. He's been handling some matters for me and I think we can probably get to see him on short notice if I explain the circumstances."

Peter Wilmot's office was in a high rise building with a spectacular view of the Thames. The young solicitor greeted Nigel and Bess warmly. The chairs he offered them were surprisingly comfortable. Often contemporary furniture sacrificed comfort for style. His office combined both.

"It looks like you had a talented interior designer." Bess commented. "I imagine I'm not the first one to say that."

"You're quite right," Peter beamed, "I'm a lucky man, the designer is my wife." Turning to Nigel, "I understand you're also a lucky man. Congratulations. My assistant told me you want to make a new will, and want it before your wedding next week. That shouldn't be a problem. I'll make sure we get to it straight away. It'll probably mean a few late nights at the office, but you'll have it."

"Peter," Bess spoke up, "I also want a will. It should be fairly simple to do, everything goes to Nigel."

"I told you, Bess, that's not what I really want, so you can change your mind." He smiled at Peter, "I told her I don't need anything. She could leave her money to her favorite charities. Are you going to help me out here and talk her out of it?'

"I'm not a marriage counselor," he joked, "And the lady looks determined. My advice to you, and this comes from a happily married man, give her what she wants."

They had agreed not to see each other in the week before the wedding.

There was a lot of preparation to complete before embarking on their voyage. They'd call only in the event of an emergency. Otherwise they would meet in one week at the dock.

Nigel stood facing the sea while he waited for Bess. He breathed in the smell of the ocean, and listened to the cry of the gulls circling overhead in their unrelenting search for food. He watched the crew making their final preparations for the voyage. The ocean liner, tethered at the dock, rocked restlessly in the harbor, as if it were anxious to break free and head for open water.

This was the only time Nigel hadn't been in charge of making all the arrangements, but he didn't think it mattered. He felt alive with anticipation, and couldn't foresee any problems. He too looked forward to open water. Being at sea had always brought him happiness.

A flower filled stateroom welcomed the future bride and groom. The ship's captain was delighted to perform a wedding for the couple who'd met on board only a few weeks ago. They were to be married privately, and then join the other passengers for dinner and dancing. The passengers had been told that they would be part of a special celebration dinner in honor of the bride and groom. Everyone on board was in a festive mood.

Bess wore a cream-colored lace dress and pinned a gardenia in her long hair. She was not a pretty bride, but she was a happy bride. Nigel was handsome in a charcoal gray suit, pale blue shirt and bright striped tie. His ice blue eyes sparkled.

The captain began the ceremony by welcoming them back on board. "I'm so honored that you chose to be married on my ship, and that you wanted me to officiate." He droned on, finally getting to the words they both had been waiting for.

"...and do you, Nigel Craxford, take Elizabeth Higgins for your lawfully wedded wife, forsaking all others until death do you part?"

"I do."

"And do you, Elizabeth Higgins, take Nigel Craxford for your lawfully wedded husband, forsaking all others until death do you part?"

"I do."

"You may now kiss the bride."

Nigel and Bess kissed.

After the kiss, Nigel surprised Bess with a small gift. It was a beautiful diamond star pendant. His hands lightly encircled her throat as he fastened the star around her neck.

Smiling triumphantly, they entered the dining room to the sound of applause. Some passengers stood and cheered the newlyweds. During their first dance as a married couple, Bess reached up on tiptoes and whispered into Nigel's ear, "I'm so glad we waited to make love until after we were married. You have no idea how much I'm looking forward to later."

He hugged her in response.

Some of the passengers talked among themselves about this seemingly mismatched pair.

"They aren't a typical couple. You'd never think a man like that would go for her, but they both look so happy. I can't imagine what he saw in her. She must be quite something to have landed him."

Bess insisted on dancing as long as the band was playing. This was her party, and she wanted to enjoy every moment. The bride could not stop smiling.

"I want to remember this night for the rest of my life," she told Nigel, who was beginning to tire.

"So do I."

"Oh you will. I can promise that." She spun him around the dance floor, taking the lead.

Only after the band had packed up and gone, and everyone else had deserted the dining room for the comfort of their beds, would Bess consider leaving. Nigel was exhausted and longed for sleep.

"You'll have that soon. Just indulge me a bit longer. I want to go out on deck and give you a surprise. Really, you deserve this."

No light penetrated the dense fog that shrouded the moon and stars. She took his hand, leading him through the darkness to their destination.

"Where are we? I don't know this part of the ship. How did you ever find this?"

"I explored the whole ship before we landed last week. When I was trying to come up with the perfect spot for your surprise I remembered this. I don't want us to be disturbed. We are newlyweds after all."

She produced two flasks. "One for you and one for me. It's my little joke, a reminder of our first conversation, or should I say my conversation. You never said a word."

"I don't need any reminder. I remember every word you said." Bess handed him his flask, touched hers to his, "To the future." They both drank. "I'm sure you do remember every word I said. So do I."

He took another drink. He was beginning to feel odd. Perhaps he shouldn't have had anything to drink when he was so tired.

"What's the surprise? You said you had one for me."

"Actually, it's a message for you." His legs were starting to feel numb.

"What kind of surprise is a message?" He was feeling confused.

"Karen Miller says hello."

"'What?"

Was he hallucinating? Did she really say what he thought he'd heard?

"You heard me. You think you're so smart. Smart enough to get away with murder. But you got caught in your own web."

Nigel grew pale. His terrified eyes tried to focus on Bess.

Nigel's screams were drowned out by the roar of the powerful engines that moved the ship through the night. Bess never heard the splash as his body plunged into the icy black water.

The widow could not stop smiling. She was glad to have spent all the money she had on a cruise instead of a flat. She had invested well.

CHANGE OF HEART

Jill saw the caller ID on her ringing phone. "Hello Eddie, how much do you want this time?"

"Jill, I haven't even told you why I'm calling."

"Let me take a wild guess, you want money."

"Yeah, but I only need enough to see me through a rough patch. Give your only brother a break."

"Thank God you're my only brother. What happened to all the other 'breaks' I gave you? The only time I ever hear from you is when you want money, which you never pay back."

"You know I'm not well," he whined, "I can't help having a bad heart. How do you expect me to work? I could get lucky and find a heart donor soon. Then I'd get a job and pay you back. I promise."

"Other people on that list who have the device you have manage to lead a pretty normal life while waiting for a transplant."

"Yeah, but if it should malfunction, I'm dead."

"And if I get hit by a truck while crossing the street, I'm dead. That doesn't keep me from doing what I need to do."

"Jill, honey, my luck is going to change. I just know it."

"If good luck was handed to you on a silver platter you'd find a way to screw it up."

"Remember your promise." Desperation was creeping into his voice. "After Mom died you said you'd take care of me."

"Of course I did. What kind of big sister would I be if I didn't say that to a ten-year-old child? And I did exactly that until you joined the Navy at eighteen. That promise wasn't a lifetime guarantee. Whenever I've relented and started feeling sorry for you, it's been a disaster. You've caused Mike and me so many arguments. I defended you and said it wasn't your fault that you had constant hard luck. You had me believing for years that nothing was ever your fault. Mike finally convinced me to take my blinders off, and when I did it wasn't a pretty sight. He saw through you. Mike said you were nothing but a parasite, and he was right."

"How can you say that? Besides you guys wouldn't even miss any money you gave to me. You and Mike have so much of it."

"Did it ever occur to you that we have so much because we've worked hard for so many years, and oh by the way, saved our money instead of spending it all?"

"I can't help being sick!"

"You know what, Eddie, I'm sick too. Sick of you. You know me, there's a lot more I could say, but I'll keep it simple, that way you might actually get it. Don't ever call me again!" With that she jabbed the off button on her phone, ending the conversation. Her heart was racing. Hanging up wasn't enough to quell her rage. She thought, "in addition to the off button, there should be a FUCK OFF button. Now there's a technological advancement!"

Eddie stared at the silent phone lying in his hand. Listlessly raising his head, he stared straight ahead. His eyes and his life out of focus. The feeble winter sun had long given up trying to penetrate his grimy windows. The air and sheets remained unchanged in the dingy apartment. He sank further into his sagging sofa, and further into despair. He knew it was useless to ever call Jill again. Attempting to make her feel guilty was futile. Once Mike had succeeded in convincing her, she'd never change her mind. Those two had grown so close over the years, that if they ever got a divorce, they'd need a surgeon as well as a lawyer to separate them.

He sat, hardly moving, long enough for the light to disappear behind a thick layer of threatening clouds. An early twilight seeped into his apartment. The storm arrived bringing a mix of sleet and snow. The sound of ice pellets pecking against the window unnerved him. He would have to face this nasty weather in order to buy food for his dinner. New York winters were not for the faint of heart, and his was weak.

Hunger drove him out of the apartment and into the storm. Bending into the wind, he thrust his hands deep into his pockets for warmth. Sleet stung his face as he slipped along on the snow and sleet covered sidewalks. Mother Nature was not always maternal. Thankfully it was only a couple of blocks to the grocery store. Passing by St. Bridget's he found himself closer to the homeless than he wanted to be. Their cardboard boxes, used as makeshift homes, littered the church steps. The men inside them shivered. He thought that for some, death would soon erase all memories of the cold. Passing an empty lot next to the church, he noticed a few scrawny bushes that had survived the scorching summer, huddled under their blankets of snow. Even the plants struggled here.

Life was not easy in this part of the city. Someone had named this borough Queens. "Where did they come up with that?" The only queens who had ever lived here were not royal. He knew that the lights of Manhattan, now hidden by storm clouds, glittered in the distance. Even though he could usually see it, he couldn't get there. It might as well have been The Emerald City. It wasn't the problem of too many miles to travel, it was the problem of too little money. Manhattan was the island of millionaires, living in skyscrapers, who could afford to look down on the rest of humanity. He felt that where you ended up in life was unpredictable. Make a right turn, step off the curb, and get hit by a car. Make a left turn, and meet someone who will change your life forever. Eddie continued straight ahead until he rounded the corner at the end of the next block. A cheerful red and white sign, 'Mr. J's', hung above the door of his destination. He entered the warmth of the brightly lit store, bringing the chill of winter in with him. The aroma of homemade food cooking in the little kitchen in back of the small store filled the air. People usually left Mr. J's with much more than they had planned on buying. Eddie's meager budget didn't allow him that luxury.

"Hello Eddie," the store's owner greeted him. A short stocky powerfully built man with thick black hair and thick features, Boris Jovanovic's unfailing good humor and warm personality made him beloved in the neighborhood. He had quietly helped out many people when he learned they were going through hard times. This had earned him a loyal following. Some came back to shop at his store even after they had moved away.

"Close the door all the way. I don't want to heat the whole neighborhood." Smiling, as usual, he waited for Eddie to tell him what he wanted, although it was always the same.

"Roast pork hero and a diet coke."

"How about some hot peppers on that? They'll warm you up."

"Nah, you know I don't like them."

"You should try it sometime, always good to try something new." He busied himself making Eddie's sandwich, smiling and humming as he arranged the ingredients on a freshly baked roll.

"How come you're always so cheerful? All you're doing is making a sandwich." This was the first time he had ever asked anything about the friendly man making his sandwich. Before this, he only talked about himself. Mr. Jovanovic always listened with sympathy and offered encouragement, assuring him he would get his transplant and regain his health. The only thing he knew about the grocer was how much he loved America.

"You see me making a sandwich. I see me making a life. I'm grateful to be in this great country. America doesn't give you anything, you have to grab it. But here you can grab it." He handed Eddie his dinner, took his money and placed it in his well-filled cash register. Even in a storm, people have to eat.

Eddie trudged back to his apartment more depressed than before he had gone out. Even an immigrant was doing better than he was. The grocer had traveled thousands of miles and found success only two blocks away. Apparently Eddie didn't know how to read the road map to a better life.

He had always relied on others to provide for him. First, of course his mother, and after her death, Jill. Then the Navy gave him meals, housing and orders to follow orders, which he never questioned. He felt more at sea now in civilian life than he ever did on any ship.

After his discharge Jill had urged him to invite some of his old friends and acquaintances over for dinner. She said it would be a good way to readjust to civilian life and to start networking. "Who knows, it could possibly even lead to finding a job. People are usually willing to help returning veterans. All you'd have to do is to make a meal."

Eddie had refused.

Jill was exasperated with his attitude. "Your problem is that you say no to everything. If you always say 'no' to life, that's what you'll get. No life."

Eddie didn't answer. After he developed heart problems, he felt his body had become his jailer. It never occurred to him that it was really his mind.

He reached the entrance to his apartment without any ideas about what his next move should be. His disability check and his left ventricular assist device were his lifelines. But neither could be relied upon to sustain him for too long or too well. He felt like the Tin Man in search of a heart. Stamping the snow from his feet, he opened his mailbox embedded in the wall of the narrow foyer. He was clearing out the usual junk mail that cluttered the box when the door from the basement that led into the foyer was pushed open.

"Eddie Gavula, just the man I was coming up to see, after I finished taking this trash outside."

"I know the rent is due. I expect my check will be in tomorrow's mail, since it didn't come today."

Walter Staab smiled, but Eddie knew he wouldn't be smiling tomorrow if he didn't get his rent. Eddie had been renting the two rooms over Staab's Hardware for almost eighteen months now. When he first moved in, he was hoping it would be a very short time before he could move to a better place, but since he did no more than hope, it never happened.

Walter Staab was the third generation to own the store. While Eddie could see that his landlord worked hard, still he resented the fact that the business had just been given to him. "Why can't someone leave me something?" he thought. But all he said was, "Tomorrow, I promise."

He entered his apartment, turned on the overhead light bulb, and searched for a clear surface to put down his dinner. The coffee table was strewn with empty containers of take-out food. The folding card table next to the Pullman kitchen held dirty dishes and a pizza box. The sink also was filled with dirty dishes. He couldn't even put the pizza box in the trash can since it was already filled. He had to settle for balancing dinner on his lap.

Tomorrow, he promised himself, he'd straighten things up. Tomorrow was becoming his favorite word, since he never accomplished anything today.

The next day, Eddie hoping the check would be there, opened his mailbox but was only half surprised that it hadn't arrived. "This always happens to me. It's not my fault. I don't control the mail. How can I be expected to pay the rent without my check?" Looking for a job to supplement his income had never occurred to him.

Remaining in his apartment for the day to avoid the landlord wasn't an option. If Walter Staab didn't get the rent, he'd knock on Eddie's door. If he didn't get an answer, he'd use his key to enter the apartment. It had happened a couple of times before. On those occasions, Eddie had returned home to find a note taped to the refrigerator door. The note gave him two options, pay up or pack up. The unwritten message was just as unsettling. There was no way he could hide in his own apartment. He had to get out now in order to avoid an unpleasant encounter with Staab.

Luckily for him, while still cold, the weather had cleared. The morning sun was melting yesterday's snow. He had no particular destination in mind, but found himself retracing last evening's route. Instead of the slippery conditions he had encountered during the storm, today his only obstacle were the stacks of newspapers piled in front of the stationery store next to St. Bridget's. He stepped over them, taking care not to fall. The delivery man hadn't even made any effort to carry them from his truck to the store's entrance.

"What's wrong with people today?" thought Eddie. "First the mail doesn't come on time, now the delivery man is too lazy to put the papers where they belong." Looking out on the world it was always easy for him to find fault. He never directed his gaze inward.

He knew he'd have another obstacle to face when the weather turned warm. It was then that the store owner's three dogs waddled out, and taking up as much room as possible, sprawled out on the sidewalk. Most people smiled as they made their way carefully around the overfed animals. Eddie always crossed the street to avoid them. He resented the fact that these animals did absolutely nothing, yet obviously never missed a meal.

Whenever he heard anyone comment that someone was 'treated like a dog,' he thought of those three. "I should be treated so well."

He rounded the corner, coming to Mr. Jovanovic's store. One glance in the window made it impossible for him to keep going. From where he stood, he could see Jovanovic talking to a tall, slender, beautiful young woman. He had to go in and see her.

"Hi, Eddie, what do you want?"

"What I want is to go to bed with this gorgeous girl," he thought. "A cup of coffee please." He was finding it hard to concentrate. She was even more beautiful up close. She had soft dark curls that peeked out from underneath a cherry red woolen cap. Her face, flushed from the cold, was calm and sweet. Wearing a cherry red woolen coat that matched her cap, she looked like a rose blooming out of season in this bright winter day. He felt his heart would have stopped just looking at her if he hadn't had his assist device. He was surprised when he saw her lean in close to Mr. Jovanovic and give him a light kiss on his cheek.

"Bye, Pappa. Thanks for watching Stroopsie. See you later."

Eddie, smitten, was disappointed she never looked in his direction.

Then she was gone, unaware that Eddie had been staring at her. Her father, however, was not unaware.

"So you like my Anna," he teased. "I see how you looked at her. You're not the only one. Here's your coffee." He handed it to Eddie who was sitting at the one small table set aside for customers who wanted to eat in the store. A funny looking, short legged, black and white spotted mutt trotted happily at his heels. When she saw Eddie, the dog backed away and started to bark.

"Quiet Stroopsie, don't be rude to the customers." The grocer smiled indulgently at the dog and took a treat from his pocket to quiet her. She stopped her barking, but moved no closer.

"My daughter's neighbor used to walk Stroopsie, but he moved away. So now I've got the dog while Anna works. Stroopsie's a rescue. Anna took one look at her and fell in love. Adopting this dog proves my girl has a good heart. She has a soft spot for underdogs. She says she gets it from me," he beamed.

"God, if she can fall in love and rescue that ridiculous looking creature, maybe there's hope for me," he thought.

"Eddie, do you have a minute? I want to talk to you about something."

"Sure, what's up?"

"I just got a call from Paulie, he slipped on some ice near his house last night and broke his ankle. He's not going to be able to come back to work for a while, so I need some help around here, especially now that I have to watch the dog. Maybe not full time, at least not to start. We can see how it goes. You told me your heart device works pretty well, and I don't think anything I need you to do should be a problem. What do you say?"

Normally he would have scoffed at the offer, since he looked down on menial work. He always imagined he'd have an important job, though he never imagined what he would have to do to get it, but this would give him an opportunity to see Anna regularly.

"What do you want me to do?"

"A little of this and that. Sweep up at the end of the day, watch the store when I have to spend time in the basement putting supplies away, or when I want to run errands. You could learn to make sandwiches for the lunch crowd, and walk the dog sometimes. In fact, if you start today I could use you to walk Stroopsie right now." Mr. Jovanovic picked up a leash and handed it to him. "OK?"

Eddie, not an animal lover, inwardly groaned. But he wasn't going to let that be an obstacle. For Anna, he would even pretend to like her stupid dog. He had never been so smitten by anyone before.

Eddie bent over and attached the leash to the dog's collar.

"How come she's named Stroopsie, did your daughter giver her that name?" Eddie thought the silly name suited the silly looking dog.

"No, that was the name her former owners gave her. The people at the pound said she was brought in by an older couple who were selling their house and moving to an apartment that didn't allow dogs. They were heartbroken to have to give her up."

Stroopsie perked her ears up at the sound of her name, then sat down, refusing to go with Eddie. Apparently the dislike was mutual. With some coaxing from Jovanovic, Stroopsie eventually allowed herself to be walked. She did what she needed to do quickly, then tugged at her leash anxiously leading the way back to the store.

Time passed more quickly than Eddie had expected. It was actually easier to work than spend the day trying to avoid his landlord.

"You've been a big help to me today, Eddie, can you come in again tomorrow?"

"Yeah, Mr. Jovanovic that'll be ok."

"Good, but since you'll be working here now, do me favor and call me

Mr. J., otherwise you'll spend half the time I'm paying you just pronouncing my name."

"No problem, but I have to ask you a favor." He explained the situation with the late check and asked for an advance so he could pay his landlord when he got home. "I should have it definitely by tomorrow, so I can give you the money when I come in then."

His new boss hesitated for a moment, then agreed.

Eddie got up his nerve to ask another favor. "Could you pay me under the table so I don't have to declare any income? I really could use all the help I can get."

The second request was denied.

"No. That I won't do. America's a great country."

"Oh no, not the America lecture again," Eddie mentally rolled his eyes.

"It doesn't give you anything," Jovanovic continued, giving his favorite lecture. "You have to grab it. But it's here to grab. My parents brought me here when I was ten years old. They gave me a chance to live in this great country, and we thanked God every day for that opportunity. When we first came here we got help from the government until my family was able to take care of themselves. Where do you think that money came from? I'll tell you where."

"I'm sure you will." Eddie thought unhappily.

"Taxes, that's where. You wouldn't get a disability check if nobody paid taxes. What I will do is work with you and show you how to get ahead by saving your money. Every time I pay you, take some of it and put it away. Then you'll never have to worry about paying the rent again. You'll need to have some put away for the time you have to be in the hospital. You don't want to come out and find you have no place to live, do you?"

Unlike Jovanovic, Eddie never planned that far in advance, so hadn't thought of that. He tried to appear interested in all this good advice. It reminded him of a conversation he'd once had with Jill after one of the many times he'd come to her for money.

"You know what some people do when they have money problems?" she asked.

"What?" he asked, eager for easy answers.

"They get a job!"

This wasn't the answer he hoped to hear.

"You can wind up living on Easy Street, there's just no easy way to get there."

Now like then, he was disappointed. And now like then, he had no other choice, not if he wanted to see Anna again. Constant thoughts of her had lodged in his mind, and he had no desire to evict them.

"That's a good idea Mr. J., you're right," he said, pretending to be grateful.

He did, however, make one more request.

"Don't tell anyone I'm on the transplant list. I don't want people feeling sorry for me and asking a lot of questions. I hope to have a bright future." But it wasn't other people he cared about, it was only Anna. It wouldn't improve his chances with her if she knew his condition.

Mr. Jovanovic nodded ok. "How old are you, thirty, thirty-one?"

"Thirty-three."

"That's very young, plenty of time for you to make it yet. I agree with you. I think you have a lot to look forward to."

Eddie did get satisfaction going into the hardware store, just before closing time, and paying his rent. He enjoyed seeing Walter Staab looking so surprised.

"You thought I couldn't pay. Don't worry about getting your rent anymore. My luck has changed, and I expect it to get even better," he boasted, and strutted out the door with an air of importance.

When Eddie caught a glimpse of himself in the living room mirror, it shocked him. It had been quite a while since he paid any attention to his grooming. His unwashed hair needed to be cut, he hadn't shaved in days, and his clothes were stained. Now he was grateful Anna hadn't noticed him when she was talking to her father.

Years ago, when he was still in the Navy, his ship had docked in some port city, he couldn't remember which one now. He had passed a second-hand store, filled with dusty old furniture. An elderly, broken down man was staring in the store window, the reflection of his forlorn face captured in an old mirror. He, like the abandoned furniture, unwanted. Eddie was reminded of that face as he saw his own reflection. The memory frightened him.

"It's not too late for me. I won't end up like that old man," he vowed.

He hadn't realized how much he'd let himself go. There was still time to bring his clothes to the laundromat and get a haircut before Hector closed his barbershop. Meeting Anna had been like shock therapy for him. He was allowing himself to hope for a future that included her.

"Anna Gavula, that sounds better than Anna Jovanovic," he mused.

But right now all he had to offer her was a shorter last name.

"Good morning Eddie, you clean up well. Why were you keeping your good looks a state secret?" Mr. Jovanovic laughed, enjoying seeing such an improvement in Eddie's appearance. He was also relieved not to have to tell Eddie that he expected him to come to work looking neat and clean. He thought he would have to bring up that subject today. It confirmed his belief in the basic goodness in people. "If you just show an interest, and give someone a chance, they can make it."

Eddie's dark brown hair was neatly trimmed, and shaving off the stubble revealed a nice-looking face. He wore a denim shirt that complimented his blue eyes.

"I thought I should look more professional if I'm going to work here."

"That's a good idea." But Mr. Jovanovic guessed that it had everything to do with Anna and nothing to do with the job. He really didn't care what the reason was, he was happy to have made a difference in someone's life. He was optimistic that he would have some part in making Eddie's life better. He also didn't worry about Anna ever being interested in Eddie. She knew her worth and would never settle for someone who was not her equal. Now with Frank Russo in her life, it was almost impossible for any man to compete. Mr. Jovanovic shook his head in pity at Eddie's unrealistic dreams concerning his daughter. He would, however, do everything he could to help him realize the ones that were possible.

He was happy that Anna had found Frank. He remembered the night she came for dinner and first told her parents about him. Anna, who taught at a local charter school, had approached Frank's hedge fund firm to seek funding for a project she wanted to start. She was nervous about trying to convince a group of high-powered people, who lived such privileged lives, to help her under-privileged students. Would they care that something as basic as nutritious food and a safe place to stay after school, where the students also could get help with their homework could mean the difference between success and failure, and in some cases, even life or death? But to her relief, the meeting had gone well.

Frank had been the one in his company who wanted to help the disadvantaged. Anna said that he asked a lot of questions that revealed both his idealism and his pragmatism. As Anna excitedly bubbled on about the meeting, her parents looked at each other knowing it was not just the success of her presentation that caused her glow.

When Anna was first introduced to the group, she got the usual reaction from the men, Frank included. It was the rare man who was not almost immediately attracted to her. But after she finished speaking she saw that he was not just attracted to her beauty, he was attracted to her.

For Frank, as a successful handsome young man, beautiful women were not a rarity in his life, but women of substance were. Frank was certain he had just met the woman he would marry.

Eddie eagerly waited for Anna. He heard the barking before he saw her. He stood by the door, making it impossible for her not to notice him. As she came in, he smiled at her. She nodded, briefly looking at him without pausing, and walked quickly to the back of the store where her father was slicing the meats and cheeses needed for today's sandwiches.

"Hi, Pappa, here she is," handing over the leash with Stroopsie excitedly jumping up to greet him. "I'm running late, see you later." Then she was gone. It would be hours before she came back.

Mr. Jovanovic glanced at the clock right after she left, and the next time he looked it was almost four. It always surprised him how quickly his day disappeared. Talking to the customers as he served them was like socializing with friends. People would walk blocks out of their way to come to his store. The place had a convivial atmosphere as everyone talked and kidded around as they caught up with each other's lives. Those who claimed that New Yorkers weren't friendly had obviously never been here. Mr. J's had become a neighborhood institution, it was even featured once on the local news when two of his customers who had met in the store wound up getting married and had the wedding catered by Mr. J's. Even though Eddie had been shopping here for many months now, he never joined in the friendly banter that the other customers enjoyed. He was irritated with all their chatter, and felt it slowed down the service. He had no interest in them, but now that he was working here he was forced to be friendly. For him, unlike Mr. Jovanovic, it seemed to take three days to get to four o'clock. Eddie thought he was doing the customers a favor by waiting on them. Mr. J. patiently explained it was the customers bringing their business to his store that made him successful. "Without them," he said, "I wouldn't be able to pay your salary. They're doing us a favor by coming here. I like to treat everyone well and have them leave happy. It's good business and costs me nothing. Look, here comes Mrs. Moscarella, go open the door for her. She likes a little pampering. You'll see how easy it is to make someone happy."

He did as he was asked, and let in a heavyset middle-aged woman. "Thank you. young man, I don't think I've seen you before. When did you start here?"

"Why these questions; why is this anything she has to know?" he wondered irritably, unaffected by Mr. J's efforts to educate him.

Mr. Jovanovic answered for him. "This is Eddie Gavula. He just started working here. He's going to help me until Paulie can come back. Poor Paulie fell on some ice, so he'll be out for a while. But tell me about you. How are you today?"

"Like me," she sighed heavily.

"Well, if you said you were like somebody else I'd have to report you for identity theft," he teased her.

Mrs. Moscarella left with a large bag of groceries and a small temporary smile.

Just as Mrs. Moscarella walked out, Slim the neighborhood drunk unsteadily swayed towards the door. No one knew his last name. He didn't seem to need one, but everyone knew his reputation; a mean drunk. The police would take him off the streets for a while, but he always returned. Eddie feared trouble. The tall, red faced drunkard, staggered slightly as he made his way to the counter. Taking off his hat as he entered, he smoothed his wispy gray hair.

"Hi Slim, how are you?" Mr. Jovanovic greeted him as if he was actually glad to see him.

Slim spoke slowly, trying and failing not to slur his words. "Not too bad. Thank you for asking."

"You want your usual?"

"Yes, please." He sat down at the little table, carefully placing his hat on his lap, and waited quietly while Mr. Jovanovic kept up a friendly one-sided conversation while he made Slim's sandwich.

After he left, Mr. Jovanovic turned to Eddie, "That man could get a sandwich anywhere, but do you know why he comes here? Here he gets respect. He's more hungry for dignity than food. He wants to be treated like a person, not just a drunkard. And do you know what, he always goes out of his way to be nice to me. I never have trouble with him. I like to give everyone who comes in here something from me that makes their lives better. If you think of others, Eddie, it makes you happier. And remember what I said before, it's good business." Mr. Jovanovic looked at him trying to see if his words had any impact.

They didn't. Knowing Anna was coming soon to pick up Stroopsie was all he cared about. He kept looking out the window anxious for her arrival.

Approaching the store Anna saw Eddie at the window. It was the first time she had really looked at him. A man his age taking a job as her father's helper could mean only one thing, she thought. "He's another one of my father's 'projects'." She smiled, thinking of her overly optimistic father. Everyone who knew Mr. J. said he was all heart. Eddie opened the door for her. He was thrilled when he saw her smile, assuming it was for him.

"Anna," called out her father from behind the counter, "Meet my new employee Eddie Gavula. He's taking over until Paulie can come back. Eddie this is my daughter Anna. I'm sorry I didn't get to introduce you last time she was here."

Eddie eagerly extended his hand.

"'Nice to meet you," she said shaking his hand, and then left him so she could speak to her father. "Thanks for helping me out. I've put an ad in the paper for a new dog walker, so I hope I won't have to bother you much longer."

Eddie panicked when he heard that.

"I don't mind walking her," he interrupted, not thinking to ask Mr. Jovanovic if that was all right with him. He came over to Anna.

"Really, I don't mind. Your dad made a place for her in back of the store, so she's not in the way. If you bring her here she won't be alone all day, and it won't cost you anything."

Anna looked at her father, surprised that a new employee would make such an offer without asking permission.

"That's a good idea, it's fine with me," her father responded, "if it's ok with you."

"I guess so, I can always see how it goes. Thank you, Eddie," she answered hesitantly.

Eddie beamed. "I'm happy to help any way I can." He rooted himself next to Anna.

"It's 5:30 you can go now."

"If you need me to stay longer Mr. J., I don't mind."

Anna looked ill at ease. Like Stroopsie, she took an instant dislike to him.

"'No, you go home. You want overtime now?" he kidded. "See you in the morning."

Eddie, happy that she had accepted his offer, walked out of the store pleased with himself and his little victory. Anna frowned as she watched him growing smaller with each step. She was reminded of her Aunt Susie, a clueless woman who was incapable of understanding anyone's feelings but her own. She would swoop down on unsuspecting little children that she met for the first time, grab them, pinch their cheeks and kiss them. She was always baffled when they began to cry.

"He's too forward Pappa. He stood so close to me, it made me uncomfortable. I don't like him. The only thing I do like is that Stroopsie won't be alone when I'm at work."

Anna couldn't help shaking her head as she compared Eddie Gavula to Frank Russo, it didn't seem possible that they were the same species. God was feeling generous the day Frank was born, lavishing him with gifts. On that day he received robust health, intelligence, compassion, integrity, humor, ambition, good looks and a loving family.

Even her father, with his tunnel vision, who only saw the light at the end, never the darkness around him, knew Eddie needed help.

"He needs polishing. Let's give it some time and see what happens."

Anna remained doubtful.

Mr. Jovanovic was pleased with Eddie's progress. He was learning the business and soon would be able to run the store on his own. Paulie was a good helper, but Eddie showed more promise. He was making an effort to be friendly to the customers, even though it wasn't his nature. Mr. Jovanovic was also pleased that business was good enough to keep both of them employed after Paulie returned to work. He encouraged Eddie to save something from every paycheck. Eddie soon had enough put aside to cover a few months' rent. But still nothing was changing for him. Anna never spent more than a few moments in the store each time she came to drop off and pick up her dog. And although he could save a small amount each week, he hid the resentment he felt when he compared it to the large amount of cash his boss took home.

"Why should he make all that money? I'm as smart as he is. I work as many hours as he does."

The light stayed longer in the sky as winter died. The bare ground in the empty lots sprouted a stubble of new growth. Weeds finding a home in small cracks and crevices in the sidewalks pushed themselves up from the dirt toward the sun, determined to survive. But for Eddie, the new season was an unwanted reminder that time had passed and hadn't brought him any closer to realizing his dream.

Boredom and bitterness filled his days. He was quickly losing interest in working if he couldn't see a way to change his relationship with Anna.

"Nothing good's going to happen. Maybe I'll quit. What's the point of going on?"

The phone rang. Mr. Jovanovic put down his cup of iced tea to answer it.

"How can he drink that stuff all day?" Everything about his job and his boss irritated him.

"Sure honey, no problem." He hung up the phone and turned to Eddie. "Anna's going to get out of work too late to pick up Stroopsie today. She lives pretty close by, so can you drop Stroopsie off at her apartment on your way home?"

Eddie was thrilled. "Ok Mr. J."

At the end of the day, puffed up with the prospect of finally getting to talk to Anna, Eddie strutted out of the store in a victory march. He had been rehearsing what he was going to say to her, planning to turn the subject to a new Italian restaurant that had opened in the neighborhood. He was going to offer to take her there. Thanks to Mr. Jovanovic's advice on how to handle money he could now afford it. Maybe he shouldn't have told her father not to tell anyone about his needing a new heart. Perhaps if she knew that he was looking forward to a future of good health and had plans in place to notify his landlord and prepay his rent when it was time for his transplant, she might be impressed by that. But, as he thought more carefully about it, he realized he still didn't want her to know he wasn't in perfect health. His hopes rose like bubbles, and like them, quickly burst. The sharp blast of a horn cut into his thoughts and ripped apart his dreams.

It was Anna, pulling into her driveway in an expensive sports car. The driver, Frank Russo, got out and came around to open her door.

"Hi, thanks for bringing Stroopsie home. I was really running late today."

Stroopsie, always glad to leave Eddie, suddenly lurched forward pulling him off balance as she ran wagging and barking to greet Anna and Frank. He felt like a fool, following this ridiculous looking dog who appeared to be leading him. They both bent down to pet her. Frank leaving Anna still fussing over Stroopsie, straightened up and extended his hand to Eddie. "Frank Russo," he said, "Thanks for helping Anna."

Eddie looked up into the face of a tall, well built, ruggedly handsome man. He was an unwelcome sight. Red faced with rage and humiliation, unable to speak, Eddie nodded and quickly left the three of them enjoying their little family reunion. He retreated in defeat. "It's his money, that's why she likes him," he told himself. "If I had money I'd have a chance." He needed money, he needed it now but had no way to get it.

Pacing around his cramped apartment, his mind raced for answers. That's when he thought of the cash her father kept hidden away when he didn't have time to go to the bank at the end of the day. It would be simple to get in, since he had been entrusted with a key for the times he needed to open the store. There was no alarm. Mr. J., a man of unfailing optimism, didn't think it necessary. This would be easy. His fingerprints would be expected to be everywhere, so that wasn't an issue. He knew where the money was hidden, but would open the cash register and rummage through the store to make it appear that the thief didn't know where anything was. He'd use his key to enter and break the lock when he left. When he came to work tomorrow he'd act shocked about the theft. Confident that nothing would go wrong, he relaxed and waited until it grew too late for anyone to be out on the streets.

He entered the back door unseen. The store, brightly lit and cheerful by day, looked unfamiliar. Like his childhood bedroom it was strange and ominous in the dark. He remembered his favorite toys casting long shadows that fell across his bed, terrifying him even as he hid under his blankets. The streetlight shining in the storefront created strange shadows that distorted reality. The chair appeared to have a person sitting in it. The familiar noise of the day was missing. No hum of traffic, no horns honking impatiently, no children's voices calling out, no chatter of people passing by. Night sounds could be heard in stark relief against a backdrop of silence. The clock on the wall ticked, loudly marking the passing of life. A low hanging branch pushed by the wind, scraped against the sidewalk. Eddie started. A police siren sounded in the distance, then faded, as it headed in another direction. He feared his pounding heart would wake the neighbors.

"Calm down," he told himself. "Nothing's going to go wrong." He approached the cash register, about to break it open, when he thought he heard footsteps in the basement. He walked quickly towards the noise, putting his ear against the door to reassure himself it was imaginary; no more real than the person he had seen sitting in the chair. But as he looked down, a sliver of light beneath the door reignited his fear. The footsteps, now on the stairs, grew louder. This was not his imagination. The door started to open. Eddie, sweating and shaking in panic, threw his body against it, then ran out into the quiet night. The sudden slamming of the back door woke a neighbor's dog that started barking in frantic alarm. Eddie did what he always did when he got in trouble, he ran. He forced himself to slow down, and walked home as quickly as his pounding heart allowed.

Entering his apartment, he leaned against the door, breathing heavily, trying to keep out what just happened.

"What did happen?" he questioned himself. "Nothing," he convinced himself.

He hadn't been seen. The back door locked automatically, leaving no evidence of a break in. Nothing was disturbed or missing. He shut the basement door before whoever was opening it came out. No crime was committed, no harm was done. Still his heart was beating dangerously fast. Going to his medicine chest, not turning on the light, he reached for his tranquilizers. In the dark, he wasn't sure how many he took. Quickly, he fell into a dreamless sleep.

He slept through the incessant barking of the neighbor's dog that woke its owner. He slept through the wail of the sirens of the police car responding to the neighbor's worried call. He slept through the moans of a dying man, bleeding and broken on a cold cement floor. He slept through the ambulance racing through the night trying to get to the hospital in time. He slept through the agonizing cries of Anna and her mother, when they learned their loved one was dead. He slept through the nightmare he had caused.

He did not sleep through the ringing phone. Groggily, he answered, wondering who was calling before dawn.

"This is Long Island Jewish Hospital; may I speak to Edward Gavula."

"That's me," he said coming awake with hope.

"We have a heart for you. Are you able to get here immediately?"

No matter how his fingers trembled trying to push the keypad, he had to make the call and leave his message now. Once he got to the hospital there would be no time.

"Mr. J. this is Eddie, I won't be able to come to work for several weeks. I finally got lucky. I still don't want anyone to know why. I'll give out that news when I'm ready. See you soon, I hope." He was looking forward to regaining his health and seeing the expression on Anna's face when she learned about his transplant. He imagined she would have to be impressed with all that he had endured.

The surgeon was pleased with his patient's rapid recovery. "You're a lucky man. You can go home today. You've got a great heart now, top of the line model."

Eddie laughed, "I think you're right. For the first time in my life I feel light-hearted. From now on I'm going to celebrate two birthdays every year. The date I was born and June 15, the date I was reborn. Thank you, Dr. Gerson." This was the first time Eddie had ever thanked anyone and meant it.

The fatigue the doctors told him he would experience for a while did not affect his mood. The new heart beat optimism as well as blood through his body. He knew there would be a day when he would feel better than he had in years. He looked at his dirty apartment in amazement that he had lived like this. He emptied the overflowing trashcans into plastic bags that he would take outside when he had more strength. He also wanted to paint and get new furniture after he was able to clean his small apartment. He fell asleep happily making plans.

He waited several weeks before going to Mr. J's. His recovery was going so well he expected to be able to return to work within a month. He couldn't wait to tell Anna and see the look on her face when she learned about his transplant. Walking to Mr. J's he remembered that winter day he had returned home so depressed. It had been hard for him to face the contrast between his own life and that of the successful grocer's. Then he couldn't imagine anything working out for him, now he couldn't imagine anything not.

He smiled and nodded to people he passed on the street. Everyone seemed to be enjoying this sunny summer morning. A woman coming out of an ice cream parlor held four different flavors of ice cream cones, like a frozen bouquet, in her hands. Her excited children clapped and laughed. He found himself laughing with them. The intense heat that would rise from the sidewalks in waves would come later in the day. Now he enjoyed a cooling breeze.

As he entered the store he saw a tall woman behind the counter. She was a heavier, older version of Anna, comfortably settled into middle age. "Hello, you must be Anna's mother."

"You know my daughter?"

"Of course. I worked here. I was away for a while, but I'm back now. I'm Eddie Gavula. Does your husband ever mention me?"

Mrs. Jovanovic's eyes suddenly filled with tears. "My husband is dead."

"WHAT?" Eddie asked astounded. "When did this happen? How did it happen? I'm so sorry."

"Recently. He had an accident. I can't talk about it, it's too painful. I'm sorry."

He sat down in shock, not knowing what to do. What did this mean for his plans to come back to work? Would he see Anna again? But his next thoughts were only of poor Mr. Jovanovic, and what would be best for Anna. This was not the time to try and win her heart, when hers was now as broken as his had been. This was the time to provide whatever comfort he could to a devastated family.

"Mrs. Jovanovic, I know you don't know me, but I would be happy to come back to work if that would help. I can start in a few weeks. Please consider my offer. I used to help Anna too, by walking Stroopsie."

The little dog lying down in her favorite spot in the back room, heard her name and trotted out. She saw Eddie, barked, wagged her tail and licked his hand. He was amazed at her reaction. He was more amazed at his own. He liked it.

"If Stroopsie likes you, you're ok. I could use someone to help me here. You can start whenever you want."

Though he longed to see Anna, he just sent his condolences. The day he received the good news that he was fit enough to resume normal activity, he called Mrs. Jovanovic to tell her he'd be at work in the morning.

The first few days he was back at work, he missed Anna. She dropped off Stroopsie before he arrived and picked her up after he had left. He wasn't upset, he knew he would see her eventually. His new-found patience surprised him. He was glad that Anna insisted that her dog was good company for her mother. "I don't want you alone in the store, and Paulie can walk her."

When Anna did appear, it was the end of the day. She was surprised to see him.

"Eddie, I didn't know you were back. Thank you for your thoughtful note. It was very kind of you to think of me."

Eddie couldn't tell her she was almost all he thought about.

"Your father was a wonderful man. I know this was a terrible loss for you."

"He was the.....", then Anna went silent. She, like her mother, was too distraught to talk about it. All she could do was to pat his arm in gratitude. Her mouth quivered like a lost child trying not to cry.

Tears blurred Eddie's vision. He wanted to ease her suffering, but felt helpless. Anna looked at Eddie wondering why he seemed different. The Eddie she remembered seemed only interested in himself. His obvious concern caused a fresh eruption of her barely controlled emotions. Now she was like a lost child who could not stop crying. Instinctively she went into his arms for comfort. He held her gently, and they cried together. Her head lay against his chest, her tears soaked his shirt. He breathed in the scent of her soft curls brushing his face. He was amazed that the moment he had dreamed of for so long was finally happening. Amazed that this beautiful woman was in his arms at last. Amazed at the tenderness he felt for her. Amazed at his need to comfort her. But was most amazed that he had lost all desire for her.

Were his medications causing a loss of libido? No one had mentioned that possibility. He was grateful for all the positive changes in his life. But since he had to be on these medications for the rest of his life, this was troubling.

Anna, now calmer, came out of his arms and took both of his hands in hers in a final gesture of gratitude. He looked down and saw a large diamond ring on her finger.

"You're engaged? Is it to Frank Russo, that man I met?"

"Yes," she nodded. "It happened only hours before my father's accident. He liked Frank. But now he'll never know we're getting married. I know he wanted that, he always said that Frank was good for me."

"He was right. He'll be good for you." Eddie said, meaning it. He no longer recognized himself.

Frank convinced Anna to still get married on the date they had picked the night they became engaged. "It'll be nine months after your father died. I don't think it's too soon. Besides, don't you think the best thing for your mother is to give her grandchildren? You'll be thirty by then and if we want to start a family right away, we shouldn't delay."

"Maybe you should just look for a younger woman."

Frank acted as if he were seriously considering the suggestion. Then both laughing, they called her mother and told her to start shopping for a dress.

Arriving early, Frank entered the church, glad to leave the gusty winds of March behind. Winds that rattled flimsier structures could not penetrate the solid stones of the old building. It was part sanctuary and part fortress against the world. Frank found peace and certainty in the unchanging doctrines of the Church. How grateful he was that Anna had agreed to be married here, this place he had known from childhood.

Anna, gathering up her long skirt, ran from the limousine into the foyer of the church before the rain that was gathering in the low clouds was released onto the city streets. The sounds of the organist practicing filtered through the closed doors of the nave. Soon the candles would be lit and the guests would be arriving. They would admire the beauty and enjoy the fragrance of the flower-filled room, well protected from the coming storm.

Anna paced nervously in the small bridal chamber. She was on edge but didn't want to burden her mother with her doubts. She already knew what her mother would say. "Wedding day jitters. Everybody gets them." But Anna knew this was more serious. She opened the door to call to her mother waiting outside. "Mom, is Eddie here yet? I need to see him for a moment." Eddie had always had a calming effect on her since that day they held each other and cried.

Minutes later he softly knocked on the door. "I'm here, Anna."

She opened the door at once. There was no time for prologue. "Eddie, I'm scared."

"Of what?" He listened for her answer.

"That I'll lose Frank. I'm not sure I can do this. Everyone in there is waiting for me to make my sacred vows before God. Father Sullivan will ask Him to look down on us and bless our marriage. I'm afraid once Frank is mine God will take Frank away from me like He took my father. How can I trust God after He's taken so much from me?"

"Anna, who's in there?" he tilted his head towards the closed doors. "Frank, your mother, your relatives, your friends, Frank's family. They all love you. That's a lot for one person to have. And who gave you all this, besides the wonderful father you had for many years? If these aren't gifts from God, I don't know what is. Can't you have faith in Him who has given you so much? If your father could speak to you now what do you think he would say?"

Anna relaxed, "Probably just what you said."

"Besides, are you brave enough to face the flower girl and tell her she's not needed?"

Anna, knowing that Kayla, Frank's high-spirited, four-year-old niece, had been trying on her dress and twirling around in front of her mirror for weeks now, started smiling.

"No, you're right, I'm not."

Rain, riding the heavy winds that made umbrellas useless, drenched all those unlucky enough to be outside. But in the ballroom, crystal chandeliers showered sparkling light on all those lucky enough to be at the wedding; the sound of the fierce winds drowned out by the laughter and chatter of the guests. Toasts were made, glasses clinked, waiters scurried among the crowd offering drinks and hors d'oeuvres, as a jazz quartet played in the background.

The dancing started immediately after Anna and Frank's first dance as Mr. and Mrs. Russo. The guests, celebrating this happy marriage, hoped this marked the end of sadness for the Jovanovics. Some of them would even celebrate with Anna and Frank on their fiftieth wedding anniversary.

Irene Jovanovic approached the dancing newlyweds and whispered to Anna. "Your father wanted this for you."

"I know," she answered and whirled away in step with Frank.

After dinner, Irene accompanied by a woman about her own age, approached Eddie at his table.

"Eddie, this is Eva Kessler, Boris's sister. Eva, I'd like you to meet Eddie Gavula." They shook hands. Eva gave him a questioning look, then turned to her sister-in-law, "Did you already introduce him to me at the store? He seems familiar."

"No, he hadn't started working there yet."

After a short conversation, Eddie noticed a young woman sitting alone, abandoned by everyone at her table when they had gotten up to dance.

"Excuse me," he said to the two ladies, "That girl needs a dance partner," and he quickly left.

"What a nice young man Irene. I can see why you rely on him so much. He seems very considerate."

"He is. I don't know what I'd do without him. After Boris died, one of the suppliers tried to take advantage, claiming he was owed money. I didn't know anything about it. Eddie overheard him and straightened everything out. Boris, thank goodness, trusted Eddie enough to train him to run the business. Boris wanted to open another store, he wanted Eddie to manage this one. He's become almost like family to us."

After the dance Eddie returned to the two women who were talking quietly, their eyes focused on a fine featured, young man, in his twenties. Not wanting to interrupt them he remained silent.

"When have Evelyn and Joe not had problems with Joey? When has he not made poor choices? He dropped out of college, never keeps a job. He's nothing like the rest of the family." Irene looked at her cousin's son. Hair slicked back, a foolish widow in tow, he glided across the dance floor like a well-oiled gigolo. In his search for easy money and instant gratification, he gave little thought to his future and even less to his health. He laughed at people who urged him to give up cigarettes. The smoke that hung in the air around him was so thick you could almost push it aside like a curtain. No one could convince him that he was speeding on a one-way road to self-destruction.

Eddie's expression didn't change, but inwardly he cringed in embarrassment. "That's probably what people used to say about me," he thought, remembering what he had once been. "I guess I looked as foolish as he does. Where would I be without Mr. Jovanovic? Thank God he gave me a second chance." Turning to Irene, he asked, "Do you think all he needs is someone to point him in the right direction, give him some guidance? What about hiring him to work at the store? I've been thinking it might not be a bad idea to have a delivery service. It could expand the business. A lot of supermarkets are doing it. People are so busy today they hardly have time to shop. It's pretty low risk for us, if he doesn't work out, we can always hire someone else."

Irene was pleased. "You sound like Boris."

'It's not surprising. He spent a lot of time mentoring me. I guess I finally got it." What he didn't admit was that he had learned those lessons only after Mr. Jovanovic's death.

The weeks after the wedding passed uneventfully; it was a time of happiness and healing. Eddie, pleased with his increasing vigor and his ability to make the business more profitable, was no longer in search of easy money. It was also a time of healing for Anna and Irene. Though neither of them felt ready to talk about how Mr. Jovanovic died, they were finding more reasons to smile than to cry. Anna still came to drop off and pick up Stroopsie, but Eddie knew this was just an excuse to visit her mother every day while she could. She and Frank had bought a home on the water in Oyster Bay, and were moving in after Anna finished teaching at the end of June. Anna had spoken to him about this one morning when she arrived before her mother did. "I was worried that she would be lonely after we moved to the new house, but she seems better now. We told her there's a guest cottage on the property that we're renovating. It's hers if she wants it. Mom said she'd come for visits, but wants to stay in her house and work in the store. She said it makes her feel close to my father when she's here. She also said she couldn't do it without you. You really have become like family to us."

Eddie, who also felt like he belonged with them, remembered how emotional he had become when she said this. He had reached for his cup of iced tea and took a long drink, giving him time to regain his composure. "I feel the same way."

Eddie was eager to share the story of his transplant with Anna and Irene, but didn't want to talk about himself yet. "Let them have more time to heal their own wounds." He still looked forward to seeing the expression on Anna's face when she learned about it. As May was coming to an end, Eddie decided to celebrate on June 15, the day he considered his second birthday.

He would ask them to stay at the store after closing time, and surprise them with cake and champagne. It would be the perfect opportunity to explain why he had two birthdays. About a week before the 15th, he gave them notice that he needed to talk about something, and asked them to stay after work that day. Anna also had something she wanted to talk about, and the year after her father died was the perfect time. She planned to announce that she was expecting a baby. That would soften her mother's pain on the anniversary of her husband's death. The more time she spent looking forward to her first grandchild, meant less time looking backward to her husband's death.

On the 15th, Eddie set the table in the store for his little celebration. He brought two folding chairs for the table so all three of them could sit down together. He told them that this was going to be a celebration, but before he could bring out the champagne and birthday cake, Irene stopped him.

"I have something to say also, and I'd like to say it before you tell us why we're celebrating. I never could talk about Boris's death before. I wasn't ready. But this has been a year of healing, and Eddie, you've been a big part of that process. Of course, Anna's marriage to Frank has been wonderful, and he's been so kind to me. Now I feel like there is a lot to look forward to." Anna smiled at that.

"Boris died in an accident exactly one year ago today. He went to the store late at night, he had trouble sleeping and said he might as well go to the store and bring up several big boxes of groceries from the basement so he could stock the shelves. I pleaded with him not to go so late at night, but he told me not to worry and wouldn't be gone more than a couple of hours. I went to sleep and then was woken up by a call from the police. They said Boris had had an accident and that I needed to come to the hospital. I called Anna, and we rushed to Long Island Jewish Hospital. They did everything they could to save him, but he didn't make it." Irene stopped talking for a moment, but was able to continue. "The police told me they found Boris at the bottom of the basement stairs, a big box of groceries had fallen on top of him. It looked like he stumbled at the top of the steps and the weight of the box probably made him lose his balance and fall backwards. They checked out the whole store. There was no forced entry, no sign of a break in, nothing was disturbed, no sign of foul play."

Eddie, engulfed in a growing sense of horror, started to tremble as he listened to the details of Mr. Jovanovic's death.

"Even after he died," Irene now spoke tearfully, "he was still helping people. He donated his kidney, his eyes and his heart."

In overwhelming anguish, Eddie relived the night of the failed burglary. The night he ran out of the store before he could hear the awful sounds of a man falling to his death. "No, no," he thought, "it's not possible, it can't….." Eddie fainted.

When he regained consciousness, Anna and Irene were worriedly hovering over him. "Call the hospital," Irene directed Anna.

"No," Eddie said, "call the police."

He would finally see the look on Anna's face when she learned about the transplant.

MIRROR IMAGE

Mark woke to an empty bed.....again. Fighting his overwhelming desire for sleep, he forced himself to get up in search of Jenny. Yawning, he staggered down the curving staircase. Shuffling over the highly polished wooden floors, his eyes became accustomed to the darkness. The light would not appear in the long windows for another hour. Passing the living room and library without a glance, he knew where he'd find her. Lately Jenny was always in the sunroom before the sun, sitting in her favorite chair staring distractedly at the predawn sky.

Until the nightmares started, Jenny wouldn't wake up until Mark had left for the hospital and the twins, now in eleventh grade, were on their way to school. Enjoying the silence of an empty house, she brewed her coffee filling the kitchen with its aroma, and pouring it into her mug went to the sunroom. Following her was Abby, a short-legged long-haired cat eagerly awaiting the opportunity to settle her soft warmth onto Jenny's lap. Content to begin the day together, Abby purred for the both of them.

Only later would Jenny go into her home office to write her popular advice column for the local newspaper. ASK ME was becoming so successful it was being considered for syndication. Her friends teased her, calling her Dear Abby.

"No," Jenny joked, "I'm just Jenny, that's dear Abby," pointing to her little cat serenely strolling through the house she thought she owned.

When Jenny and Mark first saw the house, it was this room that made them decide to call it home. They saw the morning sun streaming into the woods that backed onto the lawn and felt heaven itself was beaming its approval. Home had always been a happy refuge from a hectic world.

She heard him coming in behind her. In a moment she would be wrapped in his arms. "Jen," he spoke softly. "Is it the same dream?" He reached down to hold her.

"Yes, I don't know what's going on with me. What can it mean? There's nothing I can think of that should cause me to keep having it. Do you think Laura is right that it's fear of growing old, being separated from my youth?"

Mark remained silent for a while before answering.

"I know I was the one who recommended her as a therapist. She has a great reputation at the hospital, but as long as I've known you, that's never been an issue. You're a realistic upbeat person. You don't manufacture problems. Maybe because I'm so close to you, I can't be the best judge of this, but her explanation just feels wrong."

Jenny started to shake and cry. "It's getting worse. This time the dream was even more terrifying. It started out the same way. I'm about three years old, looking in the mirror wearing a new party dress. I'm very happy because I've been told I'm going someplace special. I put my arms straight out in front of me to touch my reflection, when suddenly the image in the mirror starts to scream and reach out to me, trying to pull me into the mirror. Someone, I can't tell who, is grabbing her from behind and pulling her away. Usually in the dream she just screams, this time she was screaming "HELP ME, HELP ME!" But it wasn't a child's voice, it was an adult's. Then the mirror went black. That's when I woke up. I couldn't sleep after that."

"Nobody could." Mark helplessly tried to reassure her. "Maybe you ought to talk to your mother and find out if anything traumatic happened when you were a little girl."

"Do you really think I should talk to Mom now? She just got back from Aunt Ellen's late last night, Besides, I don't want to give her more problems now that she's finally starting to recover from Dad's death. None of this makes any sense. I had such a happy childhood. Mom and Dad were always there for me. Even though I was an only child, I never felt lonely."

"I know, but you had a checkup, nothing showed up on that. Therapy isn't working. I'm out of ideas." Mark held his head in his hands.

"Neither of us can keep going on like this."

Jenny reluctantly agreed. "I've been so grateful that Mom's been in Palm Beach these past several weeks and hasn't seen what's happening here, but I'm out of options. I'll call her later and see if in spite of her coming home late last night she can see me this afternoon."

Of course she knew her mother would want to see her. When had she ever not been there when Jenny needed her? She combed her short blonde curls, and put on makeup to hide her haggard face, hoping her mother wouldn't notice how these nightmares were affecting her.

Jenny saw her mother smiling and waving at the window as she pulled into the driveway. Putting on her sunglasses, she hesitated a moment before getting out, and trying to delay the moment which she knew would upset her mother, slowly walked to the front door. Her eyes welled with tears as she remembered herself being a young girl, fueled by energy and excitement, eagerly running up this long driveway. Her mother, always happily waiting for her with cold milk, warm cookies, and endless patience.

"Hi Mom."

"What's wrong? You look terrible. You're too skinny. Are the boys all right?" Her mother, no longer smiling, anxiously questioned her.

"The boys are fine. Mark's fine, well sort of. It's me."

"Are you sick?" Always unable to disguise emotion, panic showed on her face.

"No, I'm not sick, but I'm worried. I've been having the same nightmare lately. It's wrecking my sleep. It's wrecking my life. I'm so exhausted and tense now, I can't function."

"Have you.....?"

Jenny interrupted before she could finish, knowing what her mother would say. "Of course I've talked to Mark, and I've been going to therapy and I've had a checkup. I'm at the end of my rope. Mark said maybe you knew something that happened in my childhood that could explain this. God knows I can't think of anything. Unless I've been fooling myself, I always thought it was perfect. I never even minded being an only child. You and Daddy were the best parents anyone could have." She started crying, "That's what makes this so hard. If there's no problem, what's there to fix?"

Gently pushing back the hair that had fallen onto Jenny's tear-soaked face, she stroked her daughter's hair, hoping it would soothe her as it had when she was a child. "Sit down. I'll make us some tea, then you can tell me about the nightmare."

Listening to the cups and saucers clattering on the counter in the sun filled kitchen while her mother made tea was reassuring: restoring her equilibrium that had been lost while adrift on this sea of uncertainty.

Her mother seemed more relaxed as she placed their tea and cookies on the table, thinking that she had always been able to make things come out right for her daughter. "Have you thought of e-mailing ASK ME for advice?"

"Very funny Mom. Thanks for trying to lighten the mood, but I've actually had to take a leave of absence for a while. My assistant is filling in for me for now, but I can't afford to let that go on too long or I'll lose my job."

Sitting down, she took Jenny's hands in hers and smiled encouragingly. "Now tell me about your nightmare."

"Ok, here goes." She looked down at her mother's hands holding hers and started to talk. When she finished, her mother's hands were trembling, her mouth a thin line drawn across her face. She looked away from Jenny.

"Oh my God, you know what this means, don't you?" Jenny shrieked. "What is it? You've got to tell me!"

She turned back to face her daughter and barely audible, spoke the words she never wanted to say. "You were adopted."

Jenny froze in shock, her mind clogged with questions, unable to speak. "There's more," her mother continued. "You have a twin sister."

The words slammed Jenny's heart. She struggled for breath.

Her mother pressed on, "Before I say anything else, you have to know that Dad and I couldn't have loved you any more. No matter who gave you life, we gave you love.

"When we realized we couldn't have children we were heartbroken. It took time for us to recover but after a while we decided to adopt. Because Dad was a pediatrician, we knew we wouldn't have any trouble getting approved. Everyone loved Dr. Aronson. He was also on the board of the Jewish Home for Orphans and saw how well the children were cared for, so of course we dealt with them. When we saw you we knew we had found our daughter. We then learned that you had a twin sister who had just been adopted by another family. They were coming to get her in a few days. Dad and I begged the orphanage to let us take her too. We didn't want you to be separated from your sister. We even offered to help the other family financially if they would agree, but they refused. The Home wouldn't separate you at first, but after no one wanted to take two children they decided it was better for the both of you to find good homes separately rather than staying in the orphanage together. Time was running out since the two of you were approaching your third birthday. Everyone feared that once you were past three you'd be much more likely to remember what happened to you. No one wanted to risk that.

"Dad and I originally planned to tell you about being adopted when you got older, but the struggle you two put up when you were pulled apart was heart wrenching. You didn't stop crying for days. After that we decided not to say anything that could make you feel you didn't belong with us. You're a mother, you know when your child is in pain it's the worst. You'd do anything to protect your child." She averted her eyes, unable to face losing her daughter's love.

Tears of shock spilled from Jenny's eyes, emptying her of months of uncertainty, and a lifetime of certainty.

"Can you forgive me?" her mother sobbed. Jenny's long, tearful embrace gave her the answer she prayed for.

She called Mark from the car. "You were right about my mother. Can you come home now, please?"

"They're not my real parents. I'm not who I thought I was. A lot of things in my past make sense to me now, thoughts that just came and went through my mind that I dismissed. Now I know why there weren't any baby pictures of me. My mother told me they were lost in moving. When I asked who in the family I looked like my mother told me I was the image of her grandmother. Of course there weren't any pictures of her either. When I told her I was expecting twins, she had a very odd expression on her face, almost disturbed. When I commented on it she said she was just very surprised, that's all."

Mark was greatly relieved to have an answer at last. An answer he felt would heal Jenny.

"I know this is a shock, but I think this is really good news. It proves nothing's wrong with you. Something's triggered that memory. This doesn't change the life you had. Your parents were wonderful. Their love for you was real. Everything they did for you was real. My parents are my real parents and I still wish I was adopted. I hate the thought that I'm related to them."

It was true that anyone who knew Mark and his parents well, were convinced that such a good man couldn't possibly be related to the shallow selfish people who barely bothered to raise him.

"And just because you don't know who your birth parents are doesn't change you at all. You're still the most incredible person I know. That's the real you."

Mark was right. Knowing the cause of the nightmares did put an end to them, allowing Jenny to heal. She slept well for the first time in months, delighted to see both the early afternoon sun flooding her bedroom, and Abby patiently waiting for her to get up. Yawning and stretching luxuriously, knowing the curse was gone, she smiled. It could be effortless to resume life as it had been before the nightmares started, knowing Mark would want to rebook the cancelled cruise and start enjoying themselves again. He already had waited too long.

But she couldn't do that because she knew the nightmares were not a suppressed memory, but her sister screaming for help now. How could she go on with her own life until she saved her sister's?

Now that she knew the meaning of the dream there was no other choice.

I'm coming for you. I'll find you, she vowed.

The low dark clouds stalled overhead added to her sense of foreboding. What if she didn't find her sister? Followed by the equally disturbing thought, what if she did find her? Though Mark never told her what to do, she knew his childhood taught him to be wary of family entanglements. He was against exhuming the past.

She approached a small brick office building at the end of Main Street in Huntington and pushed the buzzer for M. Ryan. Though she had walked through these doors many times, never before had she been nervous or upset. Now she was the one needing help, not one of her distraught readers desperate to track a missing loved one or an errant spouse who had stopped child support. Mickey Ryan provided security for some of the biggest businesses in the New York area. He had started a detective agency after retiring from over twenty years in the NYPD. His reputation, first as a policeman then as a detective, ensured his success. He had added the security division after 9/11.

Jenny routinely called on many people for expert advice that she could pass along to her readers. Her end of the year column was always dedicated to her sources, and Mickey, grateful for her yearly thanks and praise, always made time for her in his crowded schedule.

He greeted her warmly. "Good to see you Jenny. Here's your coffee the way you like it, milk no sugar." He pushed a tall paper cup towards her, the steam still rising from its rim. Wrapping her hands around the hot cup, she savored the warmth.

"How can I help you?"

That was Mickey, friendly, to the point, and no frills. You would never find a china cup filled with some exotic brew in his utilitarian office. He looked the part of a no-nonsense cop. Medium height, trim compact build and short cropped steel gray hair. His piercing blue eyes, set off by a ruddy complexion, missed nothing.

"Mickey, this might sound crazy to a lot of people, but you've known me for years and I think I can safely say that I've always been rational and easy to deal with and........."

"Tell me what you want from me," he interrupted.

"OK, but first you should know that I tried to take care of this myself. I'm looking for someone who was adopted forty-two years ago. Not only did the people at the orphanage refuse to give me any information, they looked at me as if I needed a psychiatrist. They were tactful in what they said, but I got the message."

While Jenny spoke, Mickey listened intently, his expression never changing. He had seen and heard just about everything in his long career.

"Well that's it," she sighed, feeling slightly foolish. "Is this something you can help me with?" uncertain she had been taken seriously.

He leaned back in his chair, rubbing his hands behind his neck to relieve the tension he felt after concentrating on Jenny's story.

"I don't dismiss psychic experiences. A lot of police departments ask for help from psychics occasionally, though usually they don't publicize that. I'll look into this. I'll need some more details then I'll get back to you. Just a warning though, you may not like what you find."

During the days following her visit to Mickey's office, Jenny's cheerful outlook returned.

Relieved of the horrors of the exhausting nightmares, and feeling physically well again, she regained confidence that the past had receded. She even began to question if her nightmares meant her sister was in any danger.

The day Mickey Ryan called was the first day Jenny had given no thought to her sister. There was a deadline to meet for her column and a lunch date with an out of town college friend who had texted her only that morning asking if they could meet for lunch. Then spending more time than she expected catching up with her old friend, she rushed to the supermarket to buy food for dinner.

Laden with bags of groceries, she dropped them onto the kitchen counter. Abby's padded footsteps grew louder as she scurried across the floor to greet Jenny. She loved this time spent by herself, the fleeting space between day and night, before her family came home. Happy to be alone, but not lonely.

The softness of spring warmed the twilight as Jenny opened the kitchen windows and began to prepare dinner. A breeze blowing through her garden gathered the scents of the first spring flowers and they soon mingled with the aroma of a roasting chicken. The biscuits would go in the oven later. She was grateful that her greatest pleasures were simple ones. As she sliced tomatoes for a salad, humming softly, another puff of wind pushed aside the sheer curtains and blew into the kitchen, presenting her with the fragrance of a spring bouquet, its scent familiar. 'Spring Bouquet', "of course." She smiled at the memory of the cologne she loved as a teenager. She wore perfume now, but occasionally still wore 'Spring Bouquet'. I wonder why I never realized until now how like it is to the real thing. A ringing phone demanding her attention startled Jenny out of her pleasant thoughts, an unwelcome intrusion into the quiet of her peaceful world.

"Jenny, Mickey Ryan. Can you come in tomorrow? I have news for you. How's 4:30?"

"Fine." One syllable was all she could manage.

"Great, see you then."

Jenny told the family about Mickey's call.

"He didn't give me any news on the phone, but knowing Mickey, I don't think he'd call yet if he didn't find her."

Mark became very quiet. The twins, Brian and Josh, thought it was 'cool' to have a mysterious aunt suddenly emerge from the past, especially one who was a twin like them. They were excitedly laughing and making up stories about what she would be like, never noticing they were the only ones talking. Mark took some papers from his briefcase and closed the door to his study before dessert was served.

He was in bed waiting for Jenny when she came up. Looking like a man who saw an oncoming storm but no place to take shelter, he kissed her goodnight and turned away. Reaching for her lamp, she turned off the light.

The meeting with Mickey was brief.

"I found your twin." He handed her a paper with her sister's name, home and work addresses. "She's moved around a lot and has had a difficult life," was the only comment he made. Mickey's expression gave no clue to his thoughts, but she suspected he knew more than he was telling her.

Smiling, Jenny threw her suitcase into the trunk, started her car and waved goodbye to Mark. He stood in the driveway, returning her wave but not her smile. He couldn't shake his worry. What Mickey discovered about her twin troubled him, especially since she insisted on going alone to find her.

Jenny had argued, "But that's the whole point. I think she needs help and I'm happy to give it. I think it will be easier for her if she meets just me."

Mark knew it was also what Jenny needed. She couldn't live with herself if she didn't pursue this. One of the reasons she had an advice column was to help others. She genuinely cared about her readers. It was one of the many reasons Mark loved her.

Jenny entered the address in her GPS and began her journey. She knew it would take her to the right place, but was it a place she should go? There was still no technology to tell her that. Dismissing any doubt, her optimistic nature took charge. I'll leave it to Mark to be the designated pessimist in the family, and gave it no further thought.

It was another four hours before she pulled into the parking lot of the address Mickey had given her. He said it was better to go to her sister's workplace than home since she was more likely to be there. She looked around the lot. Billy's Diner probably never had a customer who arrived in a Mercedes sports car. She laughed to herself, thinking how Brian and Josh would groan and call her a snob even to have thought that. They would realize when they were older that there had never been any snobbery in Jenny, she just spoke the truth.

Before getting out of the car she looked again at the diner. The faded sign sat at an alarming angle on the roof. She had no way of knowing that, even though it seemed it could fall at any moment, it had been that way for years. The exterior paint was faded and, in some places, had flaked completely off. She would have to walk carefully over the buckled and cracked asphalt.

Making any repairs would be a waste of money since no one would care. People came here for the cheap food. Anyone looking for ambience wouldn't be in Watkins Falls. Once a thriving town, its last factory had closed decades ago. A distant whistle warned of a fast-approaching train that would rattle the diner as it roared by on its rush out of town. Her spirits faltered. Instinctively Jenny tugged at the brim of her baseball cap pulling it further down until it reached the top of her sunglasses. A futile attempt to shield her eyes from the pain of reality.

"Getta load a what just pulled up," Jodi snickered to Hank, the short order cook behind the counter. "It's a god damn rich bitch." She watched in amazement as Jenny got out of her car. "What the hell is she doing here? Her GPS must really be fucked up. Her handbag probably costs more than I make all week."

The smells of frying bacon and hash browns that were served at Billy's all day assaulted Jenny as she entered the diner and slid into the first empty booth. It didn't seem to be the kind of place you waited to be seated. Jodi approached with a menu and a pot of coffee. She pushed the menu towards Jenny and turned over the cup already placed on the table.

"Coffee hon?" She smiled, hoping for a big tip from this one.

"Sure, thanks."

As she leaned over to pour the coffee, Jenny could smell her cologne.

"'Spring Bouquet'?"

Jodi looked puzzled. "What?"

"Your perfume, are you wearing 'Spring Bouquet'?"

"Oh that, yeah."

"I wear it too."

Jodi laughed a little too sarcastically for someone looking for a good tip. "Sure you do. I can see we have so much in common." Still laughing she turned away, rolling her eyes and shaking her head.

"The specials are in the front of the menu," she called back to Jenny, her retreating bulk encased in a dark green apron tied around a thick waist. Her slightly swollen feet nestled in new shoes. Jodi had cut off the Payless price tag on them this morning. With bright blonde hair, heavy makeup and hot pink nail polish, she was all artificial color. No one would take them for sisters, let alone twins, yet Jenny knew by her nametag this was the Jodi she had come for.

She delayed removing her hat and sunglasses and lingered over her coffee, waiting for the few lunch customers to leave before she spoke to Jodi. This was a conversation that required privacy.

Jodi came to the table. "Do you want anything else?"

"Yes. Please sit down, I need to talk to you."

Jodi startled in surprise. "What about?" she asked suspiciously, backing away. "Did someone send you?" She seemed almost panicky.

"Nobody sent me. I came because I need to talk to you. I promise it's nothing bad, quite the contrary. Please sit down," she repeated.

Jodi looked back at the reassuring presence of Hank, who was now leaning over the counter watching, and felt safer.

"Ok." She perched on the end of the booth opposite Jenny, like a bird on a branch ready to fly at the first sign of danger.

Jenny removed her hat and sunglasses and reaching into her large handbag, pulled out an envelope filled with photos. She looked directly into Jodi's blue eyes, ones that looked identical to the ones she saw in her own mirror every day.

"Do I look familiar to you? I should, we're twins." She spread out pictures, taken from the time she was three until late last year.

Jodi, now pale and trembling, silently stared at images that could have come from her own photo albums, if she had been lucky enough to travel or live in beautiful homes. It was only in the later pictures that they began to look different. While a smiling Jenny remained slender and beautiful, a defeated, worn out Jodi, overweight by her thirties, never smiled anymore for the camera, she had lost too many teeth.

Jodi jumped up and backed away. "Are you shitting me? Are you for real? Who the hell are you?" But looking at this better version of herself, she knew.

In spite of all the times Jenny had rehearsed the best way to approach Jodi, she had just blurted everything out and was handling this badly.

"I'm your sister, Jenny Harris." In desperation she spoke rapidly, her voice rising, trying to convince Jodi. "You were born May 3rd in Glen Cove, New York. You'll be 46 on your next birthday. How could I know all that if I wasn't for real? And I'll bet you never saw any baby pictures of yourself either?"

Jodi didn't move, tears spilled from her eyes. They mixed with her mascara, running down in blotches on her face.

"Are you ok." Hank now stood behind Jodi, his big hands resting gently on her shoulders.

"She's fine." Jenny answered for her.

"I wasn't talking to you," Hank snapped back. Hank and Jodi, two lost souls, had become very close.

"It's ok, Hank. She's my sister. Jenny, this is Hank. He's like family, a big brother."

Jenny extended her hand to Hank and shook his rough one that was attached to a hairy, tattooed arm. This was more family than she had been looking for.

Hank looked at Jodi's tear-stained face and went behind the counter, returning with a wet dish cloth.

"You're a mess," he said handing it to her.

"Tell me something I don't know," Jodi mumbled into the cloth she used to wipe her face.

"I didn't mean it that way honey. You know what I meant."

"I know. I'm just feeling sorry for myself again."

"How come you never told me you had a sister?"

"Maybe 'cause I didn't know."

With her face cleaned of makeup, Hank was startled by the resemblance to Jenny. "You're more than sisters, you guys are twins."

"So I've just been told."

"Hell, this is no place for a family reunion. Go home. I'll cover for you. Go on sweetie, I'll see you in the morning. Want me to pick you up?"

"I can drive her back." Jenny volunteered.

Hank turned to Jodi, to see if that's what she wanted. It was.

"Should I follow you home or do you want to come with me?"

"I'll come with you. Hank usually gives me a lift."

"Pull in there." Jodi pointed to a driveway that was more dirt than asphalt. 41 Railroad Avenue had no neighbors. On one side squatted an abandoned house, the other side an empty lot with nothing beyond that. There was no reason for the town to keep going. It stopped here.....a dead end. The small bungalow Jodi rented was even more poorly maintained than Billy's Diner. Rotting wooden steps leading to a sagging porch was the only way to reach the front door. Jodi told her the wobbly stairs to the back door were even worse. The railroad ran just a few feet behind the house. Only a rickety wooden fence separated the weed-filled, trash-strewn yard from the tracks. Low green hills in the distance provided the single pleasing view Jenny had seen since coming to Watkins Falls.

The stench of stale cigarettes, along with a fat black cat that looked like it had no intention of ever going on a diet, greeted the sisters as they entered the cramped living room. Jodi reached down and smiled as she affectionately stroked the creature.

"Abby," she addressed the cat, "meet my sister Jenny."

"Abby?" Jenny was incredulous, "That's the name of my cat."

"See, maybe we do have a lot in common?" Jodi was pleased, Jenny was not.

"What have I gotten myself into? Mark was right. I should have left the past where it belongs."

Dismayed, she looked around the living room. A decrepit sofa, almost hidden under a pile of old magazines, and a mismatched chair sat against one wall, a card table topped with an ashtray overflowing with lipstick stained cigarette butts, and two folding chairs against the other. A bare bulb hanging from above was the only source of light. The walls were a vile shade of faded green. A permanently stained linoleum floor separated the kitchen from the living room. Jodi noticed Jenny staring curiously at a small mirror hanging on the kitchen cabinet next to the back door.

"That's my security system. I can see if anyone's coming in when my back's to the front door."

"Like robbers are really going to come here," she thought sarcastically. She stopped herself, now ashamed. "What am I thinking? That's not me. I came because I knew my sister was in trouble. Who knows why she ended up like this? Hank likes her, so does her cat. She can't be all bad." She spent a few silent moments trying to hide her disapproval and convincing herself not to just walk away forever.

Hoping her sister hadn't noticed, Jodi grabbed an almost empty whiskey bottle next to the sink and shoved it into a cabinet. Then turning to the refrigerator, she opened the door to show Jenny it was almost empty, just a six pack of diet soda and leftover pizza.

"Sorry there's nothing to eat. I wasn't expecting company." She smiled at her attempt at humor.

The rumbling and screeching of a passing freight train shook the house, making conversation impossible. Jenny waited impatiently until it finally passed.

"That's fine." It was more than fine. She couldn't wait to leave. "I'll take you out."

Jodi was embarrassed by her sister's obvious dislike of her house. At least the landlord had fixed the leaking faucet last week. No need for this elegant stranger, her sister, to see more evidence of her dismal life.

The closest restaurant was Cracker Barrel. Jodi had never been to a Cracker Barrel before. Neither had Jenny. They studied the menu, avoiding conversation. Jenny broke the silence with a nervous laugh. "We are a pair. We're both scared, right?"

Jodi answered with a hesitant tight-lipped smile, self-conscious about her missing teeth. Away from the house, both sisters felt calmer. After ordering they made small talk. It was during dessert that Jenny first mentioned the nightmares that had started her search.

"Are you in trouble?"

"I was, but I think I'm ok now."

"What happened?"

"You're gonna have to stick around a while to hear about all that."

"Ok. I'm not going anywhere."

"Hey, that's the story of my life!"

"We shouldn't talk here." Jenny knew she couldn't concentrate if they went back to that house. "There's a Hampton Inn right down the road, let's go there. My treat." Jenny worried if that was the right thing to say. Jodi understood Jenny's dilemma, and though she made no comment, appreciated the kindness.

They talked all night. She wound up telling Jenny much more than she had intended. Maybe it was a mistake to trust this stranger and to believe she wanted to help her, but she was an old pro at making mistakes.

She never wanted to admit that it had been a terrible decision to marry Carl Fowler. She was sure that Jenny, who had love and security her whole life, wouldn't understand why anyone would stay in an abusive relationship.

At first Jodi's adoptive parents welcomed her as the child they had prayed for. She was a bright happy little girl who adjusted well to her new home. Then her father suddenly died. A seemingly healthy man, he collapsed and was dead before the ambulance arrived. Her mother never recovered from the shock of losing her husband and lost interest in her daughter as well as everything else in life. Jodi was sent away to live with different family members, never staying long with anyone. No one wanted another child to raise. Her only goal became to escape her unhappy situation. The job she took after high school paid just enough for her to get her own studio apartment. She dreamed of going to college.....someday.

He had come into the coffee shop on her first day. Since it was a popular hangout for cops, her friends teased her about working there just to meet men. They noticed each other as soon as he walked in. He looked in her direction and leaving the group he came in with, walked over and sat at the stool facing her. He was the only one not wearing a uniform. He was tall, good looking and approached her with the easy confidence of a man who was not unaware of his effect on women. Jodi, flustered, tried and failed to seem disinterested. Her hand shook as she handed him a menu and quickly turned away.

"Hey, I don't bite," he said, "just ask those guys," pointing to the cops he came in with. "I'm a real pussycat." They laughed in response and turned back to their conversation.

"Do you want coffee?"

"I usually have it with milk and sugar, but since you're here I won't be needing the sugar. Just stir it with your finger."

His charming smile and friendliness disarmed her. She relaxed enjoying their flirty banter.

"I never noticed you here before, and believe me, I would have."

"That's because it's my first day on the job."

"Well guess what, I've just been promoted to detective and today is my first day too. It must be a sign. We have to get together tonight and celebrate. Don't refuse or you'll be in trouble with the law."

She couldn't believe her luck meeting such an attractive guy on her first day. He was interesting, funny, and paid more attention to her than anyone she'd ever known. For the first time in her life she felt someone wanted her. Within a few months he convinced her there was no reason to wait to get married.

He punched her the first night of the honeymoon. He came into the bathroom of the hotel just as she was finishing putting on her makeup.

"Look at all this crap you left out," pointing to her cosmetics scattered on the counter top. "You never told me you were such a slob. Get this straight, you're not doing this in my house! Who are you painting yourself up for anyway? You're a married woman now, not some cheap slut." He knocked everything to the floor, not caring about all the broken glass.

"Now clean it up!"

Jodi sobbed and backed away from this angry stranger, cringing against a wall.

"I said clean it up now!" he punched her in the stomach and strode out of the room.

The next day he brought flowers, promising he'd never hit her again. "I had too much champagne. I was nervous about getting married." He was calmer for a while, but the pattern continued. He started accusing her of cheating on him, even claimed she was flirting with the mailman. "If I find out you've been with another man I'll kill you. If I can't have you nobody can." She finally ran away when she learned she was pregnant. He tracked her down, and punching and kicking her in the stomach, screamed it wasn't his child. She lost their baby. From then on she was afraid to trust again, vowing to rely only on herself.

The furious blows of an abusive husband couldn't penetrate Jodi's hardened exterior; it took the gentle touch of her sister's hand. She had broken down and relived what she had spent years trying to forget.

When Jodi finished both of them were silent. Reluctantly Jenny told what life was like for her since they were separated, knowing this would bring more pain to Jodi. When there was nothing more to say the sisters stared at each other in horror. Both overcome with the realization of what their life could have been. Jenny cried from gratitude. Jodi cried from grief.

"I'll come back for you. I promise. I have to work out the details with Mark, but I swear I'll come back and take you with me."

"No you won't. Why would Mark let me in his home?"

"You don't know him. He's a very kind person. I know he'll welcome you. It shouldn't take more than a couple of weeks to sort everything out. Can you give me a key to your house so I can get in to wait for you if you're not home?"

"Sure."

The twins hugged. Jodi watched Jenny drive away in her expensive car, back to her perfect life. She was certain she'd never see her again.

Doubt, persistent as an unwanted suitor, tormented her all the way home. She always kept the promises she made, but was this asking too much of Mark and the boys to bring her troubled sister into their lives? Was she asking too much of herself? She pictured Jodi living in their well-ordered home. Jodi was messy, she smoked, which wasn't allowed in their home. The liquor cabinet would have to be locked. Her mother would be heartbroken to see what had happened to the little girl she tried to adopt.

How would her friends react? Even Abby would be affected. The cats might not get along. Jodi told her she'd never move anywhere without taking her Abby. She knew she would never abandon her own cat yet she was wondering if she should abandon her sister. There was also the possible danger of exposing her family to Jodi's ex-husband. Carl had always found out where she lived no matter how many times she had moved. The last time had been years ago, but could anyone be certain he wouldn't suddenly reappear? Life without Jodi would be simpler and safer. She regretted her decision to delve into the past, but breaking her promise to come back would be heartless. She'd probably suffer from guilt the rest of her life. Taking her sister in was not going to be easy, nor even wise. In the past when faced with a difficult decision, she asked herself what would add the most value to her life. She often advised her readers to do the same thing. This time her emotions made it impossible to answer that question.

Carl planned his attack on Jodi well before he broke into her house. Once he found where she lived, he took his time learning all about her. He knew her routine. He knew that no one but Hank, undoubtedly her lover, came to the house. The noise of the regularly scheduled trains that ran behind her isolated house would cover any screams even if someone was passing by.

His car could be parked a couple of blocks away where it wouldn't be noticed. She had no family who would miss her. When he did enter the house the first time, he even found an old trunk in the basement where he could put her body. This would be easy.

He waited until just before dawn to jimmy the lock on her front door. Since he had been in the house before he knew the narrow stairs led to the bedroom where she lay sleeping. He came to the side of the bed and pressed the hard barrel of the gun against her forehead. His gloved hand covered her mouth.

"Good morning bitch."

Jodi's eyes stayed closed, she moaned and rolled over, still asleep.

"GOOD MORNING BITCH."

Jodi bolted awake, struggling to free herself and scream. But with Carl's strong, gloved hand pushing hard against her mouth, freedom was impossible.

"If you want to live you better do exactly what I tell you. When I take my hand off your mouth if you scream you're dead. No one can hear you anyway. You're going to call Hank and tell him you're sick. Tell him not to call or come over because you need to sleep. Tell him you're turning your phone off. Got that?"

Jodi's eyes flashed in panicked disbelief. How did he find her again after all this time? How did he know about Hank?

Jodi nodded.

Carl pressed the gun to the side of her head as he slowly took his hand from her mouth. She remained silent.

"Now that's a good girl." Carl stared at her. "You look like shit, nothing like the gorgeous girl I married. When I met you, you turned heads, now you turn stomachs. Why did you have to go and change? Why didn't you listen to me and do what I told you to? It wouldn't have to be like this if only you had. We had some good times in the beginning until you got all bitchy and disobedient.

"Why don't we go down memory lane while we wait for Hank to get up? Do you remember that bitch lawyer you got to divorce me? That man hater thought she was so tough. I loved it when she got that piece of crap paper that said I had to stay away from you. Who the hell is she to tell ME what to do? You both are controlling bitches. That was such a joke. Remember I told you that when I came after you with a gun, you'll see how much good that paper will do you. Do you still have it? Do you want to go get it now and scare me away? You can hold it up in front of you when I pull the trigger. Yeah, that'll help," he laughed.

He stopped talking and sat pointing the gun at her until the sun shone through the window and glared in her face. "Ok, show time. Make the call and I may let you live."

Jodi ended the call and obediently turned off the phone and placed it in Carl's outstretched hand.

"You did good. Now let's go downstairs and I'll tell you the plans I've made for you. But first why don't you fix me something to eat? I'm having way too much fun to rush this."

Carl, happiest when bullying and mocking, let the next couple of trains go past so he could enjoy Jodi's terror while he ate breakfast. Thrusting his coffee cup in her face, Jodi rushed to fill it again. "I shouldn't have to ask for more. I'll bet old Hank never has to ask for seconds, you just give him all he wants, don't you, slut?" Jodi, unable to control her shaking hands, spilled some hot coffee on Carl's lap, triggering a fresh barrage of insults aimed at wounding her. Then he ordered her to clean everything up. "No one needs to know what a slob you are. It might ruin your spotless reputation." The dishes rattled in Jodi's hands as she trembled and put them back in the cabinet. He checked his watch and knew the next train would soon arrive.

"Now I'll let you know my plans. There's good news and bad news. First the good news, I'm gonna walk out of here and you'll never see me again. That should bring a smile."

Hope flashed across Jodi's face. He couldn't stop himself from laughing.

"Now the bad news, you're never gonna see anyone again."

Grinning, he got up and aimed his gun.

"Time to move. You're going in the basement. There's an old moldy trunk down there that's just your size. You'll fit in it perfectly."

"NO!" Jodi backed away, "I won't move. Please let me go." Almost blind with tears, she collapsed to her knees pleading for her life.

"Oh you're going all right. Right now."

The house shook as the approaching train came right on schedule.

"HELP ME! HELP ME!" she shrieked. But no one heard her cries or the shot that ended her life.

Carl and Jenny had planned to surprise Jodi on the same day. Timing it so she would arrive at the end of her shift, Jenny stopped at the diner eager to surprise her at work. Thinking it would be like a scene from that old movie 'An Officer and a Gentleman', where Richard Gere rescues Debra Winger from a dreary life and carries her away, but instead of a handsome man coming to the rescue it would be her. Hank told her Jodi called in sick and said she probably wouldn't be in for a couple of days. She insisted that he not come to the house. All she needed was sleep. She also said don't bother to call because she was shutting off her phone, but would be back in a couple of days.

"She really doesn't want to be bothered."

"That's ok Hank. I'm going to take her home with me. I'll take care of her. She'll call you when she's better."

Carl dragged Jodi's body down the basement stairs, angry that she forced him to shoot her in the kitchen. The dull thud of the corpse bumping down the stairs unnerved him. He was edgy. Now there was blood to wipe up. It took a few hours before he was satisfied that he'd removed all traces of the murder. He knew her body would be found in the trunk, he wanted Hank to know she was dead, but by that time he'd be out of the country. They'd never find him. He was too smart. He took some downers to quiet his nerves and lay down on the sofa to wait until dark to leave. He didn't expect to fall asleep, but was just waking from a drugged stupor when he heard a car pull into the driveway.

Arriving at the dark house, Jenny knew her life was about to change forever. Once she walked in there was no going back. It would be cruel to give false hope to a woman who fortune had frowned on. The twins were like two sides of a coin flipped by fate. Jenny had landed heads up. She got out her sister's key, had some trouble with the lock, but finally it turned.

Carl lying on the sofa, heard the noise and thought he must still be dreaming, but he kept hearing noise even after he got up. Someone was trying to open the locked door.

"Who the fuck is that?" He stumbled into the kitchen when the front door opened, the dim light in the living room was switched on. He staggered towards the back door, opening it to get out, when he glanced in the mirror hanging on the kitchen cabinet. He stifled a scream. "I'm losing my mind." It was Jodi restored to her former beauty.

"I'm back. I came to get you."

"It's a nightmare." He knew Jodi was dead, her body face down locked in the trunk in the basement. But she kept shouting and coming into the house. Fleeing out the back door, unable to see in the dark, he fell down the stairs, and crashing into the rickety fence, toppled onto the tracks. A train whistle shrieked in the distance, piercing the silence of the night. Injured, unable to move, he panicked as it grew louder. The blinding headlights of the speeding train broke the blackness. Frantically he screamed. The train passed, the whistle faded. Once again all was quiet.

Jenny stopped calling when the noise of the train became too loud. She could see no one was downstairs, just Abby curled up asleep in front of the basement door.

Thinking Jodi must still be in bed, she climbed the steep stairs, calling "It's me, I'm back." At the top of the stairs she found the bedroom and bathroom both empty.

Strange, she thought. Where could she go, sick with no car? Hank's her only friend and he thinks she's here. Don't tell me I have to call Mickey again? I'm not sure I should.

She entered the bedroom thinking Jodi might have left a note in case Hank came looking for her.

A few pieces of furniture filled the cramped space, making it difficult to walk around. Next to the unmade bed was a small night table that held a full ashtray, an empty liquor bottle and a few coins. Jenny turned to leave and bumped into the table. One of the coins fell to the floor. She bent over to pick it up. Jodi's coin had landed face.....down.

MISS FORTUNE

The brightly colored flag, buffeted by strong hot gusts that swept the land, snapped violently in the air. Only later would a fresh wind from across the sea arrive to cool the countryside. The flag waved in bold contrast against a blazing sun rising in the pure blue sky. The marching band, that was to lead the parade along the promenade later in the day, was still rehearsing. Shopkeepers, hoping for a profitable start to the summer season, opened early.

Gretchen Loew excitedly placed her sign in the window, which was easily visible from the beach. But most people had no need of a sign to find THE FORTUNE TELLER. Her family had lived here for generations. The women, renowned for their psychic gifts, were in constant demand. Now it was Gretchen's turn to continue that tradition. Her mother had assured her from the time she was a child that she had the gift. It had started for Gretchen when she was seven, and only grew stronger over the years. Dreams that came true, knowing what events would happen before they occurred, knowing what was in a letter before it was opened, confirmed that she had inherited second sight. When she turned twenty-one she succeeded her mother, just as her mother had succeeded hers.

The family took pride in their ability to offer guidance to those who came to them, and were angered by charlatans, claiming to be clairvoyant; charlatans who preyed on the weak and the vulnerable. They considered it blasphemous to pretend to have a God-given gift.

The knock on the door announced her first client.

"Come in."

The door cracked open, and a cheerful pretty round face, framed by silky blonde hair, peered into the room from the partially opened door. "I wanted to be your first client. Looks like I got my wish." Ella Becker, giggling, entered and plopped her soft plump body into a soft plump chair facing Gretchen. She couldn't stop laughing.

"This is ridiculous, Ella. I know you too well." But a smiling Gretchen was delighted to have her best friend be the first person to come through her door.

Ella handed Gretchen a small shopping bag. "For you," she said, trying to regain her composure.

Gretchen reached into the bag and retrieved a small beautifully wrapped box of Belgian chocolates.

Then it was Gretchen who burst out laughing. "I see that this is your favorite brand of chocolate. I also see that you want me to share them with you. How am I doing so far?"

"Oh, you are good," Ella quipped, reaching into the opened box Gretchen offered her. "You knew I'd want to eat these. What an amazing gift you have. Since you already know my past, let's see what you can do with my future."

Gretchen became serious. "This isn't a game, Ella. If you want a reading you have to be prepared to learn things you didn't expect or even want to know."

Her mother and grandmother told her to trust her visions. They taught her the information she received would be true, but that she might not always understand its significance. Often it was like working on a puzzle. Bits and pieces would be revealed, but only later would the whole picture emerge.

Ella, always the optimist, wanted to continue.

Gretchen sat quietly for a few moments, head down, eyes closed. Then she looked up at her friend, who was eagerly waiting for the session to begin.

"You are very excited about your future." Ella nodded. "You're about to make a great change in your life." Ella smiled happily. "You're going to take a trip. You're getting married."

Ella rolled her eyes. "Come on, you know Eric and I wanted to get married since we were fifteen. You certainly remember. You told me you had a wild crush on him. It took you a couple of weeks to stop crying when you found out he liked me. So the whole world knows we're getting married, especially you. You've got to do better than that."

"Quiet!" a stern voice, one Ella had never heard before, reprimanded her.

The atmosphere grew tense. Ella struggled to adjust to her best friend's new demeanor.

Gretchen continued. "Of course, but you never set a date. You never even got officially engaged. But I see marriage soon, very soon. Oh my God, you're pregnant!"

Ella gasped. "I only found out last night. I told Eric this morning. We decided to elope just before I came here. How could you know?"

Gretchen looked at her.

"Stupid question."

"You're going to have a boy."

"Eric will like that."

"Sshh." Gretchen put her finger to her lips. "Don't break my concentration." Gretchen remained silent for a few moments. A worried expression appeared on her face. "There won't be any more children. Eric is going through a lot of changes. You may not see it right now, but it's already happening. You'll be losing weight....."

"Now I know this is ridiculous. I'm never going to diet."

"This is important. Listen to me. This is not about dieting. There's a lot more you need to be aware of. If you go through with this marriage you will be bitterly disappointed. Eric will never make you happy. Sometimes I don't understand the meaning of what I see, other times, like this, it's crystal clear. I don't like what I'm seeing."

Ella jumped up. "And I don't like what I'm hearing. You're my best friend, and this is how you talk to me."

"As your best friend, this is exactly how I have talk to you. I'm trying to save you from an unhappy life. Eric is going to be a bitter disappointed man. That's not going to be good for you or your son."

An outraged Ella challenged Gretchen again. "Are you sure this doesn't have more to do with you than me? Are you jealous because the so-called love of your life doesn't seem to be making any great effort to be with you? I noticed Hugh's still in Australia, not here. In spite of the great love affair you had in college in London, I don't see any ring on YOUR finger, or am I just imagining that?" Ella was shouting now. "I'm not going to listen to any more of this craziness. What should be the happiest time of my life is being ruined by you!" She bolted out of her chair, grabbed money from her wallet and angrily thrust it into a glass jar Gretchen kept on a table. "I have to go. I have a lot to do, as you already know," she added sarcastically. Her abrupt departure was punctuated by a slamming door. Gretchen called after her, but her voice couldn't reach Ella through the door that she had shut between them.

Gretchen was stunned. Her blue eyes filled with tears. Her first reading, and she botched it. A lifelong friendship destroyed in just moments, some gift. This felt more like a curse. She was busy the rest of the day and had no time to think about what to do with Ella, but from that experience she learned to be very careful discussing her visions with her clients. The rest of the day was uneventful. Her clients were impressed with her ability to see what was happening in their lives, and no one was upset by her predictions. Only the last young man troubled her. After his high school graduation, she saw nothing, just, dark, empty space. She didn't know if this signified the end of his life, or just her inability to see his future. She now knew the truth could be said in many ways. Not wanting to alarm him, she said, "I see you always young and strong." She suspected the worst, but hoped she was wrong. The young man walked away happy, unaware of his fate.

Gretchen ended her day completely drained, unable to stop replaying her disastrous encounter with Ella, who was wrong in accusing her of jealousy. Gretchen and Hugh actually were engaged. They were keeping their news secret until Hugh could come here with his parents. It meant a lot to both of them to make their announcement to their families first, before telling friends.

Hugh had made her laugh the first time they met. Besides his obvious good looks, she loved his humor and even his funny Australian accent, though he insisted it was she who spoke English with a funny accent. When he learned that she was a psychic, he teased her, calling her Miss Fortune. His dark eyes sparkled with mischief and love as he claimed he proposed to her just to save her from that 'unfortunate' name.

"Who wants to hang out with Miss Fortune? You'll be much better off as Mrs. Michaels."

Just thinking about him lifted her spirits, but she wouldn't be able to see him for several months. His sister was getting married and his mother was happily involved in all the many details of making a big wedding. There wasn't any way to convince Ella that she hadn't been acting out of jealousy without betraying her promise to Hugh not to tell anyone about their engagement, even her best friend. Besides, even if she could, she knew they were never going to speak again. What good is second sight when what you see is so devastating?

She needed to clear her mind before she went home to tell her mother and grandmother what happened. They would be heartbroken. The girls had grown up together, as close as sisters. Gretchen needed to get into the open air. Being outdoors always calmed her. She made her way to the park and walked beneath the ancient trees that flanked the promenade. Years of sea winds had gnarled and bent their branches. Lost in her thoughts, she paid no attention to the twisted shadows they cast over her path, or the blaring trumpets of the marching band.

Her mother and grandmother listened sympathetically. She couldn't stop blaming herself for the rupture. "I lost Ella," she cried. Her mother took her in her arms, "From what you said, it seems Ella was already lost. Ella didn't like the message, so she blamed the messenger. You were in an impossible situation." Her grandmother agreed. "I'm afraid life is filled with impossible situations, starting at birth. No one wants to die young and no one wants to grow old. It doesn't get any more impossible than that."

The summer wore on. Gretchen grew increasingly agitated as she continued to see no future for so many of her clients: young men, little children, whole families, healthy people in the prime of life.

This made no sense. Either she was going mad, losing her gift, or the world was about to become a terrifying place. She struggled to get through her days.

One hot afternoon brought a gang of boisterous young men, barely out of their teens, already showing the effects of too many beers, too early in the afternoon. As she approached them, she experienced a completely new sensation. Though they remained seated, she felt the floor tremble beneath her, as if being stomped on by heavy boots. When it finally subsided, she remained shaken. In doing their readings, as she had come to expect, most had no future. She saw only a few surviving to middle or old age. One of the young men who had no future, brought his girlfriend back the next day. Gretchen told them their love would always be as strong as it is now. No one ever read between the lines, for that she was thankful. But the emotional toll on her was growing.

As her day ended she once more sought relief in nature, but the moist hot breath of summer enervated her and forced her indoors out of the glaring sun. Finally, the heat broke under a torrential rain. For three days rains lashed the small town, yet the water in the gutters never ran clear. As if God had tried and failed to cleanse the earth. But at least it was cool enough to sit in her mother's garden again. The brilliant colors of the flowers were subdued by the cooling twilight mist that settled in from the sea. She sat on a stone bench enjoying the stillness, broken only by a few birds reluctant to end their day. She sat, finally in peace, unaware of the spider silently spinning its web beneath the stone bench.

Gretchen went back to work with a strengthened resolve to separate her emotions from her readings. She could not change destiny. Maybe someday this would all make sense, but for now she realized her clairvoyance was her gift, her burden, her destiny. But as her days continued in the same unsettling way, her resolve weakened. Her emotions swung between doubting her ability, or being overwhelmed with dread. She desperately needed Hugh to be with her, needed his strong comforting arms, needed his love and protection. Her anxiety was relentless.

"Concentrate on Hugh," she told herself. "I'll get through this as long as I know we'll be together." It wasn't fair to burden her mother and grandmother anymore with her fears. She had to deal with this herself.

She went to the drawer where she kept one of his old rugby shirts that he'd given her. She smiled, crumpling and pressing the shirt against her heart and burying her face in his scent. She began to relax, feeling a strong presence of love and comfort. She drifted deeper into relaxation, allowing her to be the open channel that enabled her to look into the future. She looked, waiting for a clear picture. Nothing appeared. She waited. Finally, there it was, just what she had seen too many times ..... nothing, a dark, emptiness. This couldn't be happening. She wasn't concentrating hard enough. She was distracted by her fears. She fought her growing panic, trying to calm herself. "I'll try again. I need more time with this. I'm putting too much pressure on myself. I'll take a few hours to relax." The room darkened as the sun left the sky before she felt able to attempt another reading. She took a few deep breaths and looked again into the future. Again, she waited and waited. Again, nothing, only a dark emptiness.

"NOOOOO!" A shriek of anguish ripped from her throat. Her world gone, she fainted, crashed to the floor, and lay there splayed, like a broken doll.

Ella moved awkwardly around the cramped kitchen of her tiny apartment. Her growing belly made it difficult to perform even ordinary chores. Being pregnant wasn't as much fun as she thought it would be. Actually, nothing was as much fun as she thought it would be. She hadn't said anything to Eric, it would only cause another argument, but she knew Gretchen had been right. Ella missed her and had already decided to apologize. She was planning to go to Gretchen right after Eric left for work today. She looked at Eric, absorbed as usual in his morning newspaper. "I swear, you've turned into your father. A real creature of habit. Same routine every day, coffee, paper. You never pay any attention to me. You don't do a thing around here to help. You're just like your father," she nagged.

"And what's wrong with my father?" he asked belligerently, his face still buried in the paper.

Ella, her once sweet nature soured, was about to tell him. The phone rang. She answered it but never spoke, whoever was on the line did all the talking. She remained silent, looking shocked. She finally mumbled, "Of course." And hung up. Sobbing, unable to speak, she collapsed into a chair.

Engulfed by grief and guilt, she howled like a wounded animal. Eric glanced at her momentarily, annoyed that she was 'getting emotional' again.

Struggling to speak, she finally found her voice. "Gretchen. It's Gretchen." She shrieked. "She's dead! They found her this morning, clutching a blood-soaked shirt. She shot herself in the head."

"Sounds like she went bonkers." Eric said, still reading the paper.

"What the hell are you saying? This is Gretchen you're talking about," screamed a grief-stricken Ella.

"The same Gretchen you wouldn't speak to anymore because of the crazy fortune she told you."

"She wasn't crazy. I think she was right." She yelled. "Her funeral is Thursday at noon."

"So?"

"What do you mean, so?"

"So, means I'm not going."

"I can't believe it. Why?"

"Because there's a guy I've been hearing about who's coming to the union hall to speak. He's supposed to have a lot of new ideas how to make this country great again. We need someone who really wants to shake up the old order and bring in some fresh blood. That's why! That's who I was just reading about here." He waved the paper in her face.

"Can't you see him some other time? If he's as good as you say, he'll be making speeches all over the country. He'll be back. You'll have another chance to hear him."

"Maybe, but I'm seeing him Thursday." Eric threw down the paper and stomped out of the room.

Ella, still crying, couldn't believe his reaction. She picked up the paper, curious to see what it said about the man Eric was so enthralled with. There was a long article praising this new dynamic force on the political landscape, urging everyone not to miss the opportunity to hear the powerful speeches of Adolf Hitler.